Readers love
SEAN MICHAEL

Daddy, Daddy, and Me

"Beautifully written, not too heavy… Everything was written with a positive look… and it was good!"

—Diverse Reader

"I recommend this book. You'll have a good time with a smile on your face at the end."

—OptimuMM

Bases Loaded

"I had a blast reading it and can't wait to read more by this author. I would definitely recommend this book."

—MM Good Book Reviews

Daddy Needs a Date

"This is a sweet romance for two lonely souls who inadvertently connect…. It's a happy ending that felt real."

—Joyfully Jay

"*Daddy Needs a Date* was a great read…. My only complaint is that the book ended."

—Two Chicks Obsessed

By Sean Michael

Published by DREAMSPINNER PRESS
www.dreamspinnerpress.com

SEAN MICHAEL
HOME
AND
HEART

D REAMSPINNER
—PRESS—

Published by

DREAMSPINNER PRESS

5032 Capital Circle SW, Suite 2, PMB# 279, Tallahassee, FL 32305-7886 USA
www.dreamspinnerpress.com

Home and Heart
© 2018 Sean Michael.

Cover Art
© 2018 Alexandria Corza.
http://www.seeingstatic.com/
Cover content is for illustrative purposes only and any person depicted on the cover is a model.

Trade Paperback ISBN: 978-1-64108-121-4
Digital ISBN: 978-1-64080-633-7
Library of Congress Control Number: 2018931470
Trade Paperback published December 2018
v. 1.0

Printed in the United States of America
∞
This paper meets the requirements of
ANSI/NISO Z39.48-1992 (Permanence of Paper).

CHAPTER ONE

SAWYER OPENED the door to his new place and stared around at the empty space. He'd rented the place sight unseen, and he had to admit it looked small without any furniture. Even with furniture it was going to be smaller than the house back… the old house. He took a deep breath.

Okay. Okay, this was going to be home now. He'd sold everything he didn't need, he'd sold the house, and he'd packed up his SUV and moved across country to Halifax.

A new house. A new start. A new life.

He wasn't going to cry. He wasn't. He was a grown man with cash and a good freelance job writing for catalogs with a side gig of writing greeting cards. Change was good. Scary, but good. Right? Right. He took another deep breath and squared his shoulders.

Sawyer opened the windows to let the air in; then he went to explore—he had a nice living area, an eat-in kitchen that was plenty big enough to cook in, a master, and a tiny second bedroom for an office. The leasing agent said it was the smallest apartment of the four, but it suited him, and the price was reasonable.

The building was an old house converted into four apartments. The bones of the place were lovely. He just hoped the other tenants didn't throw too many loud parties. Gosh, that was such an old-man thing to think, wasn't it?

Of course, he was a widower, a recovering alcoholic, and a bit of a hermit. Which made him sound ancient. But it was the mileage not the years, wasn't it?

He supposed he should do something about getting the stuff in his van into the apartment. At least a chair so he had somewhere to sit. He had a couple of lawn chairs, a foldout cot, his laptop, his books, and his kitchen stuff with him. The rest he was going to have to buy. Now that he was here without anything, it was tempting to second-guess the decision to sell everything, but his reasoning had been sound. He was starting anew, and that included leaving behind the things he'd shared with James and actually starting fresh.

A knock sounded at the door, startling him out of his thoughts.

He jumped, put his hand on his chest, then went to the door, curious. He opened it slowly. "Hello?"

A young guy with shaggy blond hair and lovely gray eyes stood there, lounging against the door. "Hey, man. I'm across the hall in 1B—Derek. Nice to meet you."

"Derek? Hello, I'm Sawyer Ham... Burroughs."

"Hamburroughs? Cool." Derek looked past him. "Dude, your place is pretty bare."

"This is my first hour, and it's just Burroughs." He didn't know why he'd stopped using James's name, but... this was part of his new start, right? Like not bringing the furniture. James would understand.

"Okay. You got stuff you need help with?" Derek asked.

"Oh, that's nice. I have the stuff in my SUV. That's all."

"Did you have a fire or something?" Derek asked, following him down the front steps.

"No." He was starting over. He needed everything. "Do you like it here?"

"I do. The guys in 2A and B are cool. And we all share the backyard, so we do grill-outs and stuff. Of course they often end in benefits, if you know what I mean." Derek gave him a wicked little grin, eyes dancing happily.

"Good to know." He hadn't had any benefits in six years. James had been ill fourteen months, and then... yeah. "I look forward to meeting everyone."

"We should do a cookout tonight. A welcome to the neighborhood one." Derek grabbed one of the boxes from the back of the SUV and headed back inside. "What do you do, Sawyer?"

He had to move fast to keep up with Derek's long, easy strides. "I'm a freelancer. Writing, mostly."

"Oh, that's cool. Did you write anything I've read?" Derek put the box down where Sawyer pointed, took his box from him, and set it down next to the first.

"Not unless you love catalogs or greeting cards. Thank you."

"I didn't even know those were things you could write. I mean, it makes sense, but I never thought about it as a job. Pretty cool." Derek headed back outside and grabbed another box. It wasn't long before Sawyer had been lapped, Derek seeming to have a boundless supply of energy. Derek was stronger than he looked too.

Maybe he was simply old and tired. Of course, he had just driven across country all by himself.

At any rate, it didn't take long to empty the car. Not at all. And without exhausting him either.

"Would you like a bottle of water?" he asked his Good Samaritan, grabbing one of the few left from the case he'd started his journey with and offering it to Derek.

"Don't you have a bed?" Derek asked, looking at the corner of the living room where they'd piled everything.

"No. Not yet." He had what he had. And the little collapsible cot would have to do. It was better than the floor at least.

"Okay. You can come sleep in mine. There's plenty of room." Derek accepted the offered water and sat in one of Sawyer's two garden chairs, sprawling easily.

Sawyer chuckled softly, shook his head, and settled in the other chair. "Don't stress it. I'm fine."

"Dude, I can't let you sleep on the floor. That's not right." Tilting his head back, neck exposed, Derek drank down his water, his throat working.

Sawyer remembered feeling so free, so confident in his youth. Now he didn't feel like that was anywhere he belonged. Definitely the mileage.

"You need any help with anything else?" Derek asked when he'd finished his water.

"Oh, you've been so kind. I can't ask for anything else."

"You didn't ask, I offered." Derek's grin was warm, the friendship and help offered easily. This was a good man.

"So what do you do, Derek?" He could make small talk. He really could.

Derek's grin got bigger. "I invent ice cream flavors."

"Really?" Okay, how cool was that?

"Yeah, best job in the world. My uncle owns the local ice cream factory. I started working there when I was fifteen. I learned all the jobs, including flavor development, and it turned out I have a knack for it."

"That's fascinating. Seriously. What's your favorite?"

Derek didn't hesitate for a second. "Pecan caramel brittle."

"Uhn." His eyes crossed. That sounded like heaven. He wasn't even a huge ice cream guy, but he could definitely get behind a flavor like that.

"I've got some in the freezer. You wanna come over and taste?" Derek got up, looking for all the world like he expected Sawyer to follow.

"Oh... are you sure?" He didn't have so much as a can of soup in the apartment yet. He probably ought to go to the store and buy milk, eggs, and bread at least. Maybe a couple cans of tuna too. Of course then he'd have to buy celery and mayonnaise, salt and pepper, some chili. Or maybe some peanut butter and bananas would be simpler. At least for his first day or two.

"Yeah, come on. My couch and chairs are comfier than your sad lawn chairs too." Derek turned and headed out, lanky body moving with ease.

"Don't dis my furniture, now."

Derek laughed, a sort of high-pitched giggle. "When you actually get real furniture, I promise not to dis it. Well, if it's cool I won't."

"I'll have to go shopping. I'm not in a huge hurry." He had flexibility, right? And the chairs weren't that bad to sit in.

Derek led him across the wide hall and invited him in through the door marked 1B. It was neat to see that Derek's place wasn't the same as his, or even a mirror of his. He supposed it had something to do with it being a converted house rather than an apartment complex. He had to admit, the couch looked damn comfortable.

"Sit." Derek pointed at the couch. "I'll get the ice cream."

"Thanks. I appreciate it. You have a nice place."

"Thanks." Derek went to the kitchen.

Sawyer looked around, taking in the enormous TV with several game consoles beneath it in the corner. A pair of easy chairs sat in front of that, looking even more inviting than the couch he was sitting on. The room was larger than his living room, and the way the couch and coffee table were placed, the chairs and TV seemed almost like an alcove, giving the appearance of an extra space.

He liked how airy the place was. In that way it was like his, with the high ceilings and a plethora of large windows. Derek's living room even boasted a window seat.

Derek came back with a couple of cones piled high with ice cream. "You would think I'd get tired of it as I work with it every day, but I don't. I still love it." He handed Sawyer one of the cones.

"Thank you. I appreciate it." He'd have to drop something over in a day or two. Maybe some bread.

Derek sat next to him, turning to watch him. "I wanna see what you think of my favorite flavor, because I know you're going to say it's good whether you like it or not, just to be polite."

"Well, I might be evil. You never know." He licked, though, and the smoky, nutty flavor was perfect—not too sweet, creamy. God. He could see why this was Derek's favorite.

"You don't seem evil to me. And you like it." Derek looked really pleased about that.

"I love it. It's amazing." Genuinely.

"I know." Derek looked smug. "It's the best ice cream ever. I invented it."

"That's so cool. Seriously. I love that." He grinned at Derek, surprised and pleased.

"Once I get to know you, I'll make an ice cream for you. The Sawyer."

"It'll be sour apple, I bet." That amused the hell out of him, if he was honest.

"Are you saying you're a sourpuss? Or tart?" Derek asked.

"I'm hoping to be less of a sourpuss, but we'll have to see what happens." He licked around the lip of the cone, keeping drips from happening.

"So what's making you a sourpuss?" Derek asked. Nosy kid.

"Let's just say I'm making a fresh start of everything." He wasn't ready to give his whole life story to this perfect stranger. It would take more than a delicious ice cream cone for that.

"Oh, a mystery man. That's kind of sexy."

Sawyer snorted and rolled his eyes. He wasn't sure he was able to deal with being sexy, not right now. He ignored the little voice in his head that reminded him it had been almost five years since James had died and longer than that since he'd done anything sexual.

"You like video games?" Derek asked.

"I do. I haven't played in a long time." James hadn't been into them.

"I've got a sweet setup. We all get together now and then and have a night of playing. Oh yeah, let me text the guys about a welcome to the neighborhood barbecue." Derek pulled out his phone and dashed off a text, thumbs working double time.

"Oh, you don't have to. I mean, I haven't gotten set up enough to contribute...."

"So you'll contribute next time," Derek suggested easily. "We're on for six thirty."

"I... that was... that was fast."

"Everyone's gonna be home tonight, so easy-peasy." Derek had a mouthful of his ice cream, and his face went lax as he tasted it.

"How many other people live here, did you say?" Sawyer felt a little intimidated, going from totally on his own and never seeing anyone to suddenly having close neighbors and a barbecue being thrown in his honor.

"Three. Well, four now with you. This way you won't have to worry about unpacking anything to make supper, and you get to meet everyone."

"I...." He supposed he could run out and get chips and dips to contribute.

Derek tilted his head to the side, clearly waiting for him to finish what he was saying.

"I'll bring some Coke and chips."

"You don't have to do that—like I said, you can contribute next time. Sorry, but you look wiped. You should crash 'til cookout time. My bed's super comfy."

"Oh, that wouldn't.... I couldn't." How rude would that be? No matter how tempting the thought of a real bed was.

"Dude, you haven't got a stick of furniture. Are you planning to crash on those lawn chairs of yours?" Derek shook his head. "I swear my sheets aren't nasty."

"But you don't know me...." And he had the camping cot. He yawned hugely.

Derek shrugged. "We're neighbors. And you really do look like you need to crash." Derek helped him stand and led him into a dark, quiet room.

The bed was made, and Derek pulled the covers back. "Bathroom's over there." Derek pointed to a door by the window. "Have a great nap." Then Derek left, closing the door softly behind him.

Sawyer blinked a few times, but it was dark, cool, and comfortable, and his head throbbed, so he let his eyes close. Just for a minute.

Just a few.

CHAPTER TWO

DEREK THREW together a salad from a bag and brought it and the beer he'd picked up yesterday out to the deck they all shared. He put everything in the little fridge, noticing there were already sodas in there. Cool. If the new guy didn't want beer, they had options. Go them.

He was still debating going back into his place or staying out when Benny came down with a tray of foil-wrapped baked potatoes. Benny opened the grill and set them on it. Then he turned on the gas and shut the lid.

"Hey, Dee." Benny came over and slung an arm around his shoulders before kissing him on the cheek. "Luke is bringing the meat." Benny waggled his eyebrows outrageously as he said it. "So what's the new guy like?"

Derek tilted his head and offered his first impressions. "Cute, sad, with these awesome blue eyes."

"Sad? Why sad?" Luke came down the stairs, carrying burgers and dogs on a plate in one hand and buns with condiments and stuff in the other. "Is he a vegetarian?"

Derek shrugged. "I don't know. To sad and to vegetarian. He didn't say anything when I told him about the cookout."

"How old is he?" Benny asked. "And does he swing our way?"

"Yes, he's gay, but I have no idea what he's into." How was he supposed to know stuff like that—he'd only talked to the guy for like twenty minutes. He'd invited Sawyer to the cookout and had mentioned benefits, but it wasn't like he was going to pounce on the guy and say, "Come have sex with me and the two guys from upstairs."

"Oh, he's gay, is he? Was he wearing a rainbow T-shirt?" Luke was a butthead.

Derek rolled his eyes. "Some of us have gaydar that actually works, you know."

"Gaydar is a myth, numbnuts," Luke muttered.

Derek bit back his grin. Luke never could tell. Never. Big bad Luke had no gaydar to speak of. "He is. I just know." And if that wasn't gaydar....

"Well, good. He seems nice? Frank was so... grumpy." No one had been sorry to see Frank leave. It wasn't just that the guy had been a loner, but he'd pretty much hated everyone and everything and had complained bitterly about any group activities if he caught sight of them. They'd confined themselves to their apartments for their benefits, unless he'd been out.

"Yeah, he seems nice." Derek couldn't guarantee it of course, but he was willing to bet Sawyer was going to be much easier to get along with and be friendly with.

"Will he play with us?" Benny asked.

"That's all you ever think of," Derek noted.

"Oh, please, like I'm the only one."

"I don't know." Derek shrugged. "He seems really shy."

"I meant *you*," Benny told him, laughing.

"Bite me."

"Later." Benny made a lewd face, and Derek had to laugh too.

"So we have everything we need? I have buns and condiments, including the cheese, lettuce, and tomatoes. If anyone wants bacon, I have the precooked stuff upstairs. Dessert?" Luke looked at Derek expectantly.

"Uh... I've got ice cream." He always had ice cream. Occupational hazard, he supposed, though he loved it so maybe not.

Benny and Luke groaned.

"What? Ice cream is good!"

"Not every fucking time." They pounced on him together, tickling and rubbing.

Derek howled with laughter, stretching up to take a kiss from whoever he found. It was Benny's lips that closed over his, tongue pushing into his mouth. Benny's kisses were always take no prisoners. He moaned, sucking on Benny's tongue. He felt Luke's hand on his back, large and warm and simply touching him, connecting the three of them.

A soft gasp sounded, then came the noise of the door closing quickly but fairly quietly.

Oh fuck, that was the new guy. Derek pushed at Benny and Luke, then wriggled out from between them when they wouldn't back off. They were happily humping each other as he went off after Sawyer.

The door to Sawyer's place was closed—and locked when he tried the handle. Then he saw Sawyer headed toward his SUV.

Ah, no, that wasn't right. Sawyer shouldn't feel chased out of his own place. Derek jogged out after him.

"Sawyer! Dude! Please wait."

"I'm so sorry. I'm going to head to the grocery store. I made your bed." Sawyer was pale as milk, shaking visibly.

Derek wanted to give the guy a hug big-time, and he warred with his instincts, not wanting to freak Sawyer out any further. "We were just playing around. We'll get the food cooking and just hang out, yeah? There's plenty. The grocery store can wait." Finally, he couldn't hold himself back, and he stepped into Sawyer's space and gave him a hug. He wasn't big like Luke, but he felt like it, wrapped around Sawyer's slender body. "I'm sorry if we upset you."

"No. Of course not. I'm family. I just shouldn't have interrupted."

Well, thank God for that. It hadn't even occurred to him that Sawyer was straight, and wouldn't that have been something to walk in on if that had been the case? He realized he was still hugging Sawyer, but the guy hadn't tried to step away either, so he just held on.

"You totally should have interrupted. You should have told us to put it back in our pants and make you welcome-to-the-building food already." Or Sawyer could have joined them, but his gut was saying it was going to take more than an introduction for that to happen. A hell of a lot more.

"Oh, you have been more than kind. I... I can go get something to contribute...." Sawyer still hadn't pulled away from his hug yet. And for a guy who was as pale and shaky as Sawyer had been a couple of moments ago, that was something.

Luke came out of the main door, all big muscles and dark eyes and hair, looking like a damn devil from a TV drama. "Is he okay?"

Derek rolled his eyes dramatically for Sawyer's benefit, then shifted from the hug to one arm slung over the guy's shoulder. "Of course he's okay. He was just being polite. I've let him know he doesn't have to be, as you hooligans don't know the meaning of the word."

"I'm Sawyer. Forgive the interruption, please." Sawyer held out one hand.

Luke shook Sawyer's hand, seeming to swallow it up. "Luke Desrobier. And you weren't interrupting. We were just fooling around. Are you coming back? We've got a shitload of food, and I'm starving."

"He's always starving," Derek noted. Luke worked out like a motherfucker—he was a private trainer after all, while Benny never paid attention to what he ate and worked out some, but mostly stayed fit thanks to his job as a mover for hire. Derek, on the other hand, had been blessed with a great metabolism and could eat whatever and not worry about it.

"I...." Sawyer looked a little panicked. "I don't have anything to share." It was obviously important to the guy that he contribute.

"So you can provide a thank-you for the welcome meal for next time." Luke was clearly as unconcerned about who brought what to the cookout as Derek was, as they both knew Benny was. It all evened out in the end. "Come on, man. You want a beer?"

"No, thank you. I'm a recovering alcoholic. I've been sober for two years." Sawyer looked like he was ready for just about any response he got.

"Good for you. My mom's an alcoholic. It's been nearly three years this time. Don't worry, we've got Coke and stuff too. Hell, I think there's even bottled water. It might even be cold." Luke cackled, his easy response seeming to loosen something in Sawyer.

Derek hadn't known that about Luke's mom. Only that things were tense with his family situation. He supposed he'd assumed it was down to Luke being gay, but maybe that was only a part of it.

"Coke works," Sawyer said, giving him and Luke a smile that looked a little more together than the last one.

Benny held the front door open for them, and they trooped through the main hall and onto the patio. "Do I need to turn the burgers?"

"Don't touch the burgers, man." Luke rolled his eyes. "Rule one—don't let Benny touch the burgers."

"Don't let Benny touch any meat," Derek amended, only realizing after he'd said it how it could be taken.

"Not any? Ever?" Benny looked mock-horrified before dissolving into laughter along with Luke.

Derek giggled a little.

"Good to know," Sawyer muttered.

"Sorry. Sometimes we do our best at imitating twelve-year-olds, even though Luke's almost thirty."

"I only just turned twenty-eight, doofus."

"Like I said—nearly thirty." He dodged a swat from Luke. "And Benny's twenty-five, and I'm twenty-two. What about you?" Derek would guess a little bit older than him, but not by much.

"I'll be thirty-two next month."

"No way—I would put you at twenty-five, tops. Guys, can you believe Sawyer's thirty-two?" Derek was honestly surprised.

"Not a chance. You look like a baby," Luke noted.

"That's what my… James used to say."

"Your James?" Derek asked as he grabbed a couple of Cokes out of the fridge and handed one over to Sawyer. Damn. He'd assumed Sawyer was single and not seeing anyone. Which was a shame. Well, good for Sawyer, but a shame for him, as he'd been hoping to get much friendlier with Sawyer. The benefits kind of friendly.

"Yes. Thank you for the Coke."

"So, who's your James?" And was he joining Sawyer? That hadn't been the impression he'd gotten, but long-distance relationships were hard.

"He was my husband."

"Was?" Oh man. Divorced. That sucked for Sawyer.

"Yes."

Derek looked for a ring, but it was on the wrong hand. Weird. And Sawyer was sticking to his one-syllable answers. He was curious, but it would probably be crass to keep pushing for more information.

"Was it a bad breakup?" Benny asked. Trust Benny to not care about crassness or being polite.

"What?" Sawyer blinked, then blushed dark. "Oh no. No. He had leukemia. He died. No breaking up."

"Oh man. That sucks." Benny held his beer up for a moment, then took a sip.

"I'm sorry." No wonder the guy looked sad. "Is that why you moved here?"

"We had a whole life, and I needed to start over. Everywhere I went it was like he was right there."

Derek followed his instincts again and went over to Sawyer to give him another hug. "I'm really sorry."

"I am too, but I can't change it, so...." Sawyer sighed softly, patted his back. "We should save the burgers, yeah?"

"No worries, I've got 'em," Luke said. "There's dogs too. And we're almost ready. The baked potatoes are probably gonna be another half hour, but we can start with the meat."

Personally, Derek thought that Luke would be just as happy skipping the potatoes altogether. He wasn't exactly Mr. I Love Veggies, and unlike a lot of people, he counted potatoes as vegetables.

"Thank you for the welcome. I appreciate it. I'll contribute next time."

"We're not worried." Benny opened another beer. "We know where you live."

"Yeah. I'll have to have everyone over someday soon."

Right, when Sawyer had chairs, because right now, there was no way Sawyer could host anything but a BYOB and BYOC party, where the last *B* was booze and the last *C* was chair.

"Sure, whatever. We're easy." Benny waggled his eyebrows. "And I mean that any way you want to take it."

Sawyer chuckled softly. "I'm still in flux, with furniture and stuff. I sold everything from before."

"That's pretty brave," Derek noted. To just leave everyone and everything behind. Even if it wasn't a great situation, it still took guts to just go.

"It was necessary. The burgers smell good." Sawyer was clearly ready to change the subject.

"Yeah. Are they done yet, Luke? We're starving here." And Derek would bet Sawyer was hungrier than any of them—he knew for sure the guy hadn't eaten since he drove in, aside from the ice cream, as Sawyer had spent the rest of the afternoon in Derek's bed. Only not like how that sounded, even in his head.

Derek sort of liked the idea of the lean body in his sheets, even if only sleeping. It would have been a nummy visual. He'd been good and hadn't peeked in.

He was getting a boner just thinking about it, though, so he popped up and grabbed a couple of plates. "You want a burger and a dog, Sawyer?"

"Just a hamburger, please. Then I'll check my appetite."

"You like 'em dressed?" They had condiments but no bacon for them, though Luke had said there was bacon if people wanted.

"Can I have mustard and pickles, please?"

"You got it." Derek grabbed those out of the little fridge, along with the ketchup, and dressed Sawyer's burger, his own, and the two hot dogs he was going to eat. He handed Sawyer his plate before sitting back down next to the guy.

Sawyer sat so precise and contained—quiet, but pleasant. Derek was kind of fascinated by everything about him.

Derek listened to Benny and Luke joking around, talking about the latest *Transformers* movie like it was gold, but mostly he was watching Sawyer. He couldn't believe Sawyer was ten years older than him—the pretty blond looked like a teenager, his bright blue eyes wide and unlined.

He wondered what those downturned lips would feel like against his. He bet Sawyer would be sweet, tasty. Hell, he bet they could teach Sawyer a thing or two—Luke was something else. He was not helping his boner out at all with this line of thought. Or with watching Sawyer's mouth.

Sawyer's lips were made for sucking, that was for sure. He found himself licking his own. Damn, he wanted to lean right in and feel Sawyer's lips against his.

"You're thinking wicked thoughts, Derek," Luke whispered.

"Fuck off," he whispered back. He shifted, bringing up his right leg so his hard-on was shielded from Sawyer's gaze.

"Uh-huh. You gotta wonder why Mike and Reg decided to rent to a widower, huh?"

He frowned and turned his attention to Luke. "What? Why?" What did it matter if Sawyer was a widower? It wasn't like he was an octogenarian widower who would bitch about the music or the bed banging against the wall or anything.

"I just meant because we're so... well-suited."

"Maybe they saw something in him that you don't." Derek felt protective of Sawyer. He didn't know if it was because he'd seen Sawyer first, or if it was the sadness he felt in him or what, but he didn't want Luke and Benny to make Sawyer feel bad.

"He'll be a great neighbor regardless, I'm sure." Luke patted his thigh.

"He *is* going to be a great neighbor, I can feel it." And Derek was pretty sure it wasn't simply wishful thinking on his part.

"You want to feel *him*," murmured Luke.

He walloped his friend in the shoulder.

"What? You know it's true!" Luke popped him back.

"Shut up!" He couldn't very well retaliate, though, because Luke was 100 percent right. Derek wanted to invite Sawyer to sleep with him tonight, and he didn't want to keep his hands to himself.

His eyes went back to Sawyer.

Sawyer had finished his burger and was wandering, exploring the backyard, the shed, the little bare flower patch.

"He walks like he'd be a good lay," Luke noted.

Derek couldn't disagree. There was a sexy, loose-limbed easiness in Sawyer's gait. Something unconsciously sensual and delicious.

"You think he'd let us all pounce him?" Benny asked.

"Not tonight." Luke went over to Benny and rubbed up against him. "Come on upstairs and let me show you the new toys I bought."

"New toys?" Benny lit up. He was so easy. Of course, Derek could hardly comment—he was pretty easy himself.

"Uh-huh. Brand-new and picked out with you in mind." Luke turned back to Derek. "Come join if you get bored."

"I won't. But thanks."

"Put the potatoes away for me? We can eat them for a midnight snack."

"Sure." Derek was surprised, actually, that Benny had even remembered there were potatoes still on the grill.

He watched as Luke and Benny headed upstairs, goosing each other all the way. Their laughter faded as they went into Luke's place, the door closing behind them.

Derek shook his head and rescued the potatoes. He put them in the fridge, then put the condiments away too, and turned off the gas to the grill.

"Do you need some help? Or I could finish if you, uh, need to go," Sawyer suggested.

"That was kind of it, aside from throwing out the trash. I was thinking of going back to mine and playing some *Call of Duty*—wanna join?" He sent "say yes" vibes toward Sawyer but kept from leering or looking in any way too eager.

"I don't know. I haven't played anything in a long time."

"I'll be gentle with you," he promised.

"Maybe one game. Then I have to go unpack my cot and blankets." Sawyer's eyes cut to the flower garden. "Does anyone work in the garden? Is that something I'd be able to do?"

"Sure. None of us are into planting shit. Are you good at it?" He held the back door open for Sawyer.

Sawyer gave him a soft smile. "Yeah. I am. It's comforting."

"Yeah? Cool." He opened his door and ushered Sawyer in. "You're sleeping on one of those foldout cots, right? The kind without a mattress." Because there sure as hell hadn't been any mattresses in the SUV. "You really should sleep in my bed again tonight. You know it's more than big enough for the both of us."

"Oh, I can't impose. That would be wrong."

"It would be wrong if you were imposing, but you aren't, so it isn't. You can stay till you get your own bed. I honestly don't mind." He would even keep his hands to himself unless Sawyer made a pass. That he would definitely pick up.

"I just… there wasn't any reason to pay to move them across country, you know?" Sawyer gave him an apologetic look, which was totally unnecessary in Derek's opinion.

"Makes sense. Brand-new start and all that too." They went to his couch, and he offered Sawyer a game remote.

"Yeah. I needed it. I sold the house, the furniture, everything."

"Wow. So a real cleanup and fresh start. You sure don't do things by half." Derek turned on the TV and assumed gaming position.

"No. No, I most definitely don't." Sawyer focused on the remote, studying it.

"I think that means you'll fit in well around here."

"I hope so. I'm trying to be... to find a home," Sawyer admitted.

He wrapped his arm around Sawyer and gave him a side-hug. He hoped Sawyer could be happy here because he thought the guy needed some happy in his life.

Hell, he thought the guy needed some orgasms. Lucky for Sawyer, that was totally in his wheelhouse.

Derek leaned over, their shoulders pressing together, and showed Sawyer which buttons did what. They started playing, and it might have been a while since Sawyer had gamed, but he was back in the thick of it in no time, and they worked well together. Sawyer was willing to tease and joke, even if the jibes were far gentler than Derek was used to.

They were laughing, celebrating a win, and Sawyer looked happy, bright. Derek couldn't resist, and he leaned in and pressed their mouths together. Sawyer blinked, staring at him wide-eyed. He took it as a good sign that Sawyer didn't back off, so he pressed harder, rubbing their lips together and enjoying the way it warmed him down to his balls.

"I—" Poor Sawyer looked so confused.

He kept kissing. They didn't need to talk, and he figured Sawyer's body would kick in soon and tell Sawyer what to do. His sure was.

Come on, man. Chill. Let something feel good.

Derek reached up, tangled his fingers in Sawyer's shaggy hair, and tugged. Sawyer's lips opened right up. Oh yeah, just like that.

He slipped his tongue in, deepening the kiss, and Sawyer opened wider, let him in farther. He hummed happily, loving the taste of Sawyer as he discovered it. Sawyer melted underneath him, the lean body beginning to move in a dance older than time.

He shifted slightly, pressing down against Sawyer with about half his weight. Sawyer felt so good beneath him, moving to meet his body as he ground down against him.

"I shouldn't do this. I don't know you." Sawyer's body never stopped moving.

"We can stop if you really don't want to, but there's nothing wrong with what we're doing. We're making each other feel good." He pressed their groins together harder, enjoying the way Sawyer's trapped boner rubbed against his own.

Sawyer nodded. "Yeah. It feels amazing."

"There you go." He went back to kissing Sawyer and grinding them together. He ran his fingers through Sawyer's hair and pushed his tongue into Sawyer's mouth.

Christ, Sawyer was starving for attention, for touch. How long had it been? How bad....

He kept one hand in Sawyer's hair as he moved the other over Sawyer's body. Searching for skin, he tugged the T-shirt out of Sawyer's jeans and stroked the warm, smooth skin of Sawyer's belly. Fuck, so pretty. So damned fine.

Derek curled his fingers into Sawyer's waistband and rubbed harder. God, he needed to get their jeans open before they creamed them. Or at least before he did. He could only assume that Sawyer was in the same straits as him.

The man's belly was perfectly smooth, not even a hint of a glory trail. Was he naturally bare, or did he shave? And if he shaved, was it all over? Groaning, he pushed his fingers into Sawyer's waistband. Oh. Smooth. Bare. Jesus.

"I wanna see," he murmured against Sawyer's mouth as he worked open the top button of Sawyer's jeans. His fingers were almost trembling with excitement as he drew down the zipper.

Sawyer sucked his belly in, giving him more room to work with. "I got it lasered. It doesn't grow back."

Jesus. Jesus, that had to hurt.

"Seriously? Wow." He tugged the jeans off Sawyer's hips, dragging Sawyer's underwear down at the same time. Oh, that was a pretty prick, and just look at all the bare skin around it. Derek ran his fingers over Sawyer's skin.

"I haven't... not since."

"Haven't what?" Surely Sawyer didn't mean he hadn't had sex since his lover had died, let alone masturbated.

"Since James got sick. No one's touched me."

"Oh, baby, that's a long time to go without." Derek wrapped his hand around Sawyer's cock, sliding it slowly up and down, learning it. The thickness, the silkiness of the skin. The incredible heat.

"Uh-huh...."

Even the sweet balls were bare. He bent and licked them—he needed to know.

"Oh my God!"

That was a delicious-sounding shock.

Well, as he was here.... He licked Sawyer's balls again, then began at the base of Sawyer's cock and dragged his tongue up along it.

"Oh, dear God." Poor celibate man. That wasn't natural.

Derek licked again, then again, drawing his tongue along that hot flesh over and over, wetting the burning skin.

"You'll make me shoot," Sawyer whispered.

That was the point, so Derek opened up and took Sawyer in. He closed his lips around the head of Sawyer's cock, squeezed, then lowered his head, taking it all in. Benny and Luke were both bigger, so he didn't have any problem taking Sawyer to the root and swallowing around the head of Sawyer's cock.

Sawyer cried out, wet, bitter heat filling Derek's mouth. He took it all in—he loved sucking and the results too. Once Sawyer stopped dribbling, he began cleaning the hot flesh, licking it all over.

Sawyer sobbed softly, shuddering against him. Poor guy. He super deserved a few hundred orgasms to make up for God knew how long it had been. Derek held Sawyer's cock in his lips, sucking gently, licking so softly. The man tasted good, and he wondered if he was going to keep Sawyer hard by doing this.

"Oh.... So good. I...." Sawyer looked down and blinked, moaned.

He licked a few more times, being sure to "clean" Sawyer's slit, then raised his head, trying not to look as smug as he felt. Sawyer looked utterly debauched, totally lost in pleasure. It was a wonderful look on him.

Derek moved in and took another kiss, offering Sawyer a taste of himself. Sawyer's lips were soft, yielding, and so fucking hot. He pressed against Sawyer again, sinking into him as they kissed. He wanted more, but he didn't want to push Sawyer away either.

He undulated against Sawyer and slid a hand between them, working his own jeans open. He wanted to rub up against that pretty cock, skin on skin.

"You smell good," Sawyer whispered.

"And you taste good," he whispered back, keeping the mood intimate.

"Thank you. I—I probably shouldn't have...."

Just because he'd been married once? That seemed rather Victorian. Not to mention unfair, and if Sawyer's husband had really loved him, Derek would bet that he would want Sawyer to be happy, not locked away with a chastity belt on. Derek looked Sawyer in the eyes.

"Are you kidding? That was the best thing to happen to you in God knows how long. And now I'm going to rub off with you, and that'll be the second best. All orgasms are good, but blow jobs are better." Derek laughed and pushed his hands beneath Sawyer's shirt to rub his nipples.

Oh. Rings. Little rings. What a wonderful, amazing surprise. Like the lasered pubes. Sawyer was a kinky boy wrapped in a vanilla blanket.

"I...." Sawyer grabbed one of his wrists. "No one knows."

"Who am I going to tell? I just want to play with them. With you. I want to make you feel good." He could totally keep a secret. Especially if keeping it let him keep touching and exploring.

Sawyer slowly let go of his arm. "Right. Sorry, it's just been a long time."

"Dude, it's been forever, and that is too long." Derek gave Sawyer a smile so there wasn't any sting in his words—he didn't want Sawyer to think he was being nasty.

"Yeah. Yeah, forever is a long, long time."

"Too long. You need to feed your body." He tugged at the right ring, pulling it from Sawyer's body before twisting it slightly. Sawyer's lips parted, forming an O as he arched.

"You wanna move this to my bed?" They'd be more comfortable and then could roll over and go to sleep when they were done. He was a big fan of not sleeping on the couch all night.

"You don't mind?"

"No." He held back the duh—Sawyer needed a softer touch than he or the guys upstairs did. Probably because it had been so fucking long. Maybe because it was how Sawyer was made. There was no way to tell. But he knew he was going to be careful not to hurt Sawyer's feelings or tease too roughly.

Standing, he reached for Sawyer's hands and helped him up. Then he aided Sawyer getting his jeans back up around his hips, laughing at the two of them from pure happiness.

Sawyer was beginning to worry. Derek could tell, so he reached out, wrapped one arm around Derek's waist. Then he took another kiss before moving them to the bedroom.

"There's nothing to be worried about," Derek pointed out. "We're adults, and we're both willing, right?"

Sawyer nodded. "Absolutely. Over eighteen, and I know what I'm doing."

"Then let's get naked and get into bed, eh?" He tugged Sawyer's shirt up over his head.

Oh. There was a single long-stem rose inked on Sawyer's rib cage.

"Mmm, pretty." He traced it, sliding his fingers along it.

Sawyer's breath caught in his chest. Derek kept touching, tracing it over and over. He wondered what the story was.

"It's sensitive. I almost lost it when it happened."

"As in freaked out?" He continued touching it.

"As in, uh, I was so excited I almost came," Sawyer admitted.

"Oh! Score! That is awesome." Now he wanted to go watch Sawyer get another tattoo, watch him get a boner and go off. That would be fun.

"It was… intense, yeah."

"I don't have any tattoos, but I've always wanted some."

"Why not?" Sawyer asked.

"I don't know. Maybe I need someone to hold my hand." It sounded stupid when he put it like that, but he thought maybe that was it, that he didn't want to go through the experience alone.

"I understand that."

That made him smile, and he leaned in to thank Sawyer with a kiss. He slipped his tongue between Sawyer's lips, delving in to take another taste. He thought he could easily become addicted to it, the taste and the kisses themselves.

Sawyer's fingers twined with his, holding on gently. Unfortunately he had to let go to get them naked. He made fairly short work of it, though, undoing Sawyer's jeans once again, then tugging them and Sawyer's underwear down and off. That let him get a good look at the bare skin, and he touched gently, admiring greatly. Sawyer's cock was still eager, both hard and leaking, and Derek took a breath and made himself turn away long enough to remove his own shirt and jeans, leaving them on the floor next to Sawyer's clothing.

Then he took another kiss while walking them slowly to the bed. They stopped next to it, and humming into the kiss, Derek pushed gently. He wrapped an arm around Sawyer's back and slowly lowered him down to the mattress.

Magic. He couldn't quite believe this was happening, but it was, and there were so many things to explore. He climbed up over Sawyer, still kissing him. Moving slowly, he lowered his weight onto the man, moaning at the feeling of their bodies touching, skin on skin from their shoulders to their feet.

They fit together nicely, cocks and chests and lips. He undulated, moving their bodies together. He loved the sensation of their skin sliding, his heat bumping along Sawyer's, both of their cocks burning along his belly.

"So good," he moaned, taking one kiss after another after another. He hoped Sawyer thought so too. He rubbed them together some more, reveling in the heat they were creating together.

Sawyer was eager too, cock leaking against him, leaving little kisses all along his skin.

"You like fucking or being fucked?" Derek didn't care; he liked orgasms any way he could get them.

"I... uh... I was sort of...." Sawyer swallowed hard. "I like to take it."

"I like it all. So if you want that, we could do it. Or you could do me. Or more sucking. Like I said, I just want to make you feel good. Make both of us feel good." Derek laughed. "Aka, what do you want to do?"

"I'll suck you off. Return the favor."

He reached and rubbed Sawyer's still-hard cock. "How about we suck each other off." He didn't believe in counting tit for tat for orgasms. Things happened as they happened, and as long as everyone got their rocks off, that was good enough for him.

"I can handle that." Sawyer's smile was so... dear.

He dove in to kiss Sawyer again, drawn in by the curve of the succulent lips. Then he shifted, moving to get them into position for a friendly sixty-nine. He couldn't help but smile once he was face-to-face with Sawyer's cock again. The man had a really great cock; it was bare and stiff, not hiding anything.

He rubbed his cheek along the long shaft, then licked at Sawyer's slit. Wrapping his lips around the head, he circled the flesh with his tongue. He heard Sawyer moan, and then Sawyer began to suck too. He'd expected Sawyer to be reluctant, hesitant, but no. No, Sawyer pulled at him like a master.

He moaned around Sawyer's cock and set to sucking too, giving as good as he was getting. Hopefully Sawyer's first orgasm would mean it would take longer for the second to happen. He wanted Sawyer to enjoy it.

Sawyer took him in, sucking and swallowing over and over. The man obviously loved giving blow jobs, and Derek guessed he hadn't done that since his guy'd gotten sick either. Poor sex-starved man. Derek thought that was so sad. He could help with that. He could give Sawyer all the sex he needed. He would have smiled, except his mouth was full of Sawyer's cock.

He sucked harder and slowly lowered his head, taking more of Sawyer in. Sawyer shivered, obviously trying not to thrust up.

Derek pulled off. "It's okay. You can move. You won't choke me."

"I don't want to hurt you."

"I'll put my hand on your thigh. That way if I feel like you're going too deep, I'll push you back, okay? I want you to let go and enjoy yourself, not worry about anything." Sex was about fun and orgasms and enjoyment, not about worry.

"Works for me. You're a generous man."

Derek shrugged. He was getting something out of this too, after all.

Sawyer swallowed him down, pulling at him steadily, sucking him like there wasn't anything else to say. Derek closed his eyes and took a deep breath, simply enjoying the sensation for a moment. Then he wrapped his own lips around Derek's hot flesh again, tongue rolling over the velvety skin.

He loved the low moans, the soft brushes of tongue and lips, the hint of teeth. Those made him shudder and curl his toes. He tensed, not wanting to shove too deep into Sawyer's mouth any more than Sawyer wanted to do that to him. Moaning around Sawyer's cock, he curled his fingers into Sawyer's thigh, pulling Sawyer's leg toward himself to encourage Sawyer to start moving. It was time.

They found a nice rhythm—hard, but not too fast, both of them driving toward an end. Sucking and humping. It was the most delicious circle of pleasure. And he reveled in it. He could tell Sawyer was into it too, moaning deep in his chest, fingers grasping for him.

He managed to find Sawyer's balls and touched them, rolled them gently at first, then less carefully. He pressed behind them, finding another little ring. Such surprises! Delicious ones at that.

He twisted the ring.

Sawyer bucked up, hips rolling hard. Derek hummed around Sawyer's cock and drew harder, pulling firmly on the thick prick. Then he tugged on the ring, loving the way it made Sawyer dance for him.

Damn, that was pure need, 100 percent. Derek fed off it, sucking even harder. *Come on, Sawyer, come on.* His own pleasure seemed secondary to making Sawyer pop off again.

Sawyer was fighting him, though, trying to demand his orgasm. The force was stunning, the vibrations making him shake. He finally gave in to it, his own suction ceasing as he cried out around Sawyer's cock and shot down his throat.

Sawyer groaned, the pressure easing, slowing, relaxing. Derek hummed and rested for a moment with his mouth around Sawyer's cock but not tight, not sucking yet. He was taking a moment to revel in the orgasm he'd just had and the way his cock felt as Sawyer nuzzled it. Then he turned his focus back on Sawyer's cock in his mouth. He used his tongue on the head, giving it special attention. He wondered if the next step had been getting a ring here. Wouldn't that be something? He closed his lips over just Sawyer's slit and sucked hard.

"Fuck!" Sawyer's cry satisfied Derek deep down.

He kept up the suction, sliding a finger between Sawyer's legs to gently jostle the heavy balls. He wanted Sawyer's come in his mouth again. He wanted Sawyer to lose it for him one more time.

Derek rolled Sawyer's balls, still gentle, but with a different motion this time. Then he let his finger creep farther back, and he tapped Sawyer's hole.

Sawyer filled his mouth, a needy cry splitting the air. He swallowed Sawyer down, loving the taste of the salty come on his tongue. Humming, he pulled a few more times, then began to lick, easing Sawyer down.

"I…. Whoa. And wow." The words were breathy, almost moans.

God, that was cute.

He pressed a last kiss on Sawyer's softening cock and wriggled around until they were face-to-face again. He lay on his side and offered Sawyer a smile. "Orgasms look good on you."

"Th-thank you."

He drew Sawyer in, held him.

"How about we ditch the gaming and just stay here and watch a movie?" That way they wouldn't have to move when they fell asleep, which he had a hunch would be soon in Sawyer's case. The guy had had two orgasms, and that after a day of driving.

"Yeah? You don't mind?"

"I totally don't mind." He liked sleeping with another body in his bed, actually. It was warm and comforting, and when you woke up the next day, there was someone to share your morning woody with. "I've got all the stuff like HBO and Hulu and shit, so I'm sure we can find anything you want to watch."

"I'm easy. Nothing scary, please."

"Let's see what just came out." He grabbed the remote and turned it on, queuing up Netflix. "How about the *Baywatch* movie with The Rock?" He'd heard it was funny, and come on, who didn't love The Rock?

"Sure. He's pretty."

Bingo. Everyone loved The Rock.

"I've heard it's pretty funny too." He got the movie cued up, then hit Pause on the opening credits. "You need anything? Food? Water?"

"No. No, just your company."

That was the nicest thing anyone had said to him in a long time. "It's yours." He hit Play on the movie and took Sawyer's hand, wrapping their fingers together.

They relaxed, both of them breathing in sync. Derek had to admit that it was nice doing something easy and cuddly rather than just rolling over and going to sleep.

Sawyer laughed softly at something in the movie, and he smiled. Yeah. More than nice.

He had a feeling he was going to really enjoy having Sawyer as a neighbor.

CHAPTER THREE

SAWYER FELT like a huge slut.

He crept home in the middle of the night, cheeks burning, and then locked himself in his apartment for three days, unpacking and crying and ordering furniture online. God, what was he thinking? Fucking around with a stranger?

He heard them out on the deck, and Derek had knocked on his door two evenings in a row, calling out that they had food and Sawyer was invited to share, but then leaving him alone.

His furniture finally arrived, and thank God he wouldn't have to sleep in the fucking lawn chairs again—the cot had collapsed on him the first night. Shortly after the furniture delivery, there was a knock at the door.

This time he opened the door, thinking it was someone who'd forgotten something. But it was Derek who stood there, a small smile on his face.

"Hey, Sawyer. I saw the delivery guys leaving. Thought I'd see if you needed help setting anything up or moving anything around."

"Hey. I have furniture, yay." He couldn't shut the door, could he? No. No, he couldn't. Derek had been nothing but nice to him. And it wasn't Derek's fault he'd been such a slut. "Come on in and see."

"Cool." Derek brought a couple of pop bottles from behind his back and offered one over. "Blackberry soda from the local factory. It's really good."

"Oh, that sounds sort of magical. I love blackberries." He smiled, a little tickled that Derek remembered he was in recovery.

"They do a bunch of flavors, but this is my favorite." Derek blushed lightly. "I'm into flavors and doing things the old-fashioned way and buying local."

"Let me get a bottle opener." His house was... well, right now it was a wreck, but at least he had a sofa and a recliner now. He only hoped they were as comfortable as they'd looked online. No guarantees if you didn't get to sit on them before buying them.

"Look at all this furniture." Derek laughed. "Guess I won't have that as an excuse to invite you over again. I'll have to come right out and admit I like you and I like spending time with you."

"Thank you. I needed somewhere to park my butt." He didn't admit how nice it was to have Derek enjoy his company.

Derek sat on his couch, wiggling his ass as he sat. "Nice and comfy. I hate a hard-bottomed couch."

"Me too." Sawyer sat next to Derek, pleased to find the couch was as advertised. Soft cushions were necessary post-spankings, in his opinion. Though something a little harder wasn't bad when wearing a plug. That's what kitchen chairs were for.

"I've been knocking on your door to get you to come have supper with us out on the deck again," Derek noted.

"I know. I'm sorry. I was...." What? Embarrassed? Worried? Busy? Stressed? "I don't know. I've never had a one-night stand before."

Derek's smile was lopsided and utterly adorable. "I'm kind of hoping it's not going to be a one-night stand. You totally should have stayed that night. I make a great breakfast. And I worried about your back with you not having a proper bed to sleep in."

"Thank you. I just... it's been a long time, and it was the first time since...."

"Yeah, you'd said." Derek grabbed his hand. "You're among friends now, though, you know? We're neighbors with benefits. Although the guys upstairs can be intense."

He remembered intense. "I appreciate it. Really. I was aching, obviously."

"Well, I hope you want to do it again. I like you. I liked being with you. I liked...." Derek shrugged. "Well, I liked sitting and watching a movie with you too. It was relaxing and cool."

"It was. Seriously. So, I have a dresser, a bed, and all this. I need to decide where it goes."

"Well, I'm not much of an interior decorator. But I'd be happy to help shift stuff once you decide where everything needs to be. Hell, the boys would help too if anything is super heavy."

Oh, maybe he shouldn't have asked. "I'll think about it for a while, then see what happens."

"Okay." Derek regarded him for a long moment, then noted, "You're a very private person, aren't you?"

"Am I? I guess so. I don't know." He was a bit of a broken person, he thought. He worried a lot.

"And maybe sad? I've heard your laugh—it's great, and you should do it more often. And you can tell me to go fuck myself if I get into your personal space too much. My last boyfriend said I didn't know the concept of personal space."

"I can see that. It's... sometimes I could use being brought out of my shell. Maybe."

"Yeah?" Derek beamed. "Then I'm your man."

Sawyer took another swig of the soda, swallowing hard. "This is good stuff."

"It is. So are you going to come have supper with us tonight? We'll even let you provide the meat, if you want."

"If I'm not too sore from moving furniture, sure."

"That's what you've got me for—making sure you don't get sore from moving furniture. There's much better things to get sore from."

"You know it." He had to agree, because dammit, it was true.

The little grin Derek gave him was entirely coconspiratorial. He found himself smiling back like the world's biggest dork.

"You know... we could...." No. No, they didn't need to make out. He had furniture to move. "I need to get this stuff set up."

"Or we could baptize them first." Derek's grin deepened. "Test them out. So to speak."

"We can't just... can we?" Was he that much of a slut? God knew he wanted to.

"Why not?" Derek asked. "I mean, we like each other, and I know you enjoyed the other night as much as I did."

"I did. I liked it a lot."

Derek put his bottle down on the floor next to the couch, then took Sawyer's out of his fingers and set it down too. He shifted until they were as close as they could be, touching along one side. He exhaled, barely noticing he'd been holding his breath. Then he leaned in, bringing their lips so close there was only the barest bit of air between them. "Do you want to kiss me?" Derek asked.

"Uh-huh." Sawyer shivered, moaning softly.

"Good." Derek closed the rest of the distance between their mouths, lips landing on his. He opened up, inhaling Derek's breath. It was sweet, like ice cream, and sweeter still was Derek's tongue as it slid into his mouth. Derek brought one hand up to cup his cheek, tilting his head to the side as he deepened the kiss. Soft and heated, they explored each other, Derek's free hand settling on his thigh.

"You can touch me," Derek said softly. "I won't break."

"I'm not selfish. I'm sorry." He was used to waiting for permission. He needed to let that go.

"I never thought you were—it's just been so long, eh?" Derek stroked his face, the touches sweet and comforting.

"Years. A lot of years." He reached out, sliding his hands up Derek's chest.

Derek's eyes went heavy-lidded, and he licked his lips a couple of times. "That makes me so sad for you. And it makes me want to give you a thousand orgasms to make up for the drought."

"I'm going to have to learn about everything again."

"It sounds like fun when you put it like that." Derek kissed him again. Then he lay back, bringing Sawyer with him, putting him on a living mattress made up of warm skin and lean muscles and hard bits in all the right places.

"Oh." Oh, that was delicious. His body responded immediately, his cock filling and his abs going tight.

Derek hummed, sounding totally happy with his responses. Dragging his hands along Sawyer's back, Derek touched him through his T-shirt, warming him.

He hoped he wasn't being too much of a slut, but he didn't want to stop.

"Is skin okay?" Derek asked. He tugged Sawyer's T-shirt out of his jeans without waiting for an answer, hands hot as they brushed Sawyer's skin. "God, you feel like silk. I love how bare you are. It's delicious."

"Thank you. It's permanent." Had he said that already?

"That's so fucking sexy." Derek drew his top off and tossed it on the floor. "I could get used to touching you." Derek slid his hands along Sawyer's spine, almost seeming to count each segment as he came across it.

"I could get used to your hands," Sawyer whispered.

"Yay!" Derek laughed softly, and the sound was caught between them as their mouths met again, filling him. Filling their kiss.

Yeah, he totally was a slut. No question.

"So glad you moved in," murmured Derek against his lips, hands sliding down into his jeans to grab his ass.

A part of him whispered that it could have been anyone, but he let that go. He was the one who was here with Derek, his cock rubbing against his zipper as Derek rocked them together.

It was a welcome sting, and he groaned and pushed back, humming against Derek's lips. Moaning, Derek deepened the kiss, squishing his lips between his own teeth and Derek's. That sting was welcome too, and he bucked up, rocking for a second.

"You make everything so sexy." Derek slid a leg around the back of his, hooking it there with his ankle.

"Do I?" He liked to hear it, whether or not it was true.

"Uh-huh." Derek took his mouth again, tongue slipping in to slide against his.

He stroked Derek's skin, his hands fascinated by the warm flesh. Derek had a lovely six-pack, but it wasn't super hard like he worked out all the time. This was from living and playing, from being active.

Derek moaned softly as he continued touching. He closed his eyes and focused on drawing more of those sounds out. Derek fed them to him, one after another, as he felt up the smooth skin and the rangy muscles. He groaned, answering Derek's need with his own.

"Fuck, you're an addiction," murmured Derek. "The way you feel so deeply and want so strongly."

"I missed this. Being with someone." He missed being someone's.

"I can't imagine going that long without being intimate with somebody. I'm not a slut or anything. Well, okay, I guess maybe I am a little bit. I'm gonna shut up now." Derek closed his lips together tight.

Sawyer began to chuckle; then he started to laugh, tickled.

"Sure, go ahead and laugh at me." Derek was grinning, clearly not upset.

Then Derek dug those long fingers into Sawyer's ribs, tickling him. Sawyer shouted and wriggled, trying to get away, and they rolled together, landing with a thump on the floor, Derek supporting Sawyer's body.

Derek snickered; then he started laughing too, wrapping his arms around Sawyer. Every time the giggles slowed, they'd look at each other and begin again.

Finally, Derek sighed and collapsed back onto the floor, bonking his head pretty solidly, judging by the sound. "Ow."

"Dork." Sawyer snorted, then rested his head against Derek's shoulder a minute.

"That's better than slut, I suppose." Derek giggled for a moment, chest moving beneath Sawyer, then quieted again. "You know, for christening your couch with sex—we kind of failed spectacularly."

"A little bit, but that's okay. It makes for a good story."

"That's cool—that we have a story together." Derek continued to touch him, fingers sliding randomly on his skin.

"It is, isn't it?" How did they have a story together already? Him and this sweet, sexy guy.

"Yeah." Derek drew his legs up, cradling Sawyer between them. Both hands landed on his ass, Derek squeezing. His hips rolled into the touch like they had a mind of their own. Derek did it again, this time pushing up slightly to meet his roll. "Mmmm."

"You're inspirational," he whispered.

Derek beamed at him "You're not so bad yourself, Sawyer."

Then they were kissing again, bodies moving, quickly finding the need they'd been experiencing before they'd gotten sidetracked by laughter. They tugged at each other's clothes, pulling restlessly, randomly as they tried to get naked. Their kissing wasn't helping any, but Sawyer couldn't make himself stop, and Derek didn't seem inclined to either.

"You two are something else." A low voice came from the back window, and Sawyer gasped and rolled away, grabbing his clothes.

Sitting up, Derek looked at the window. "Benny! Shit—way to be a creeper!"

Sawyer scrambled up and yanked the curtains closed. "God... I'm sorry."

Derek got up, and ignoring the fact that his shirt was still off and his jeans were open, he came over to slide an arm around Sawyer. "For what? You didn't do anything wrong."

"Except close the curtains!" came Benny's voice from outside.

"Go away, Benny." Derek didn't seem that fazed by their voyeur. "If you want to talk, knock on the door like a real person."

"I...." Sawyer tugged his shirt closed. He was burning up with mortification.

Derek drew him away from the window. "I think he was jealous."

"God, I can't believe I did that with the curtains open." He had before. In fact, he and James had done a lot of things in public before, but his life was new now.

"It was the back window. The only guys who would see are Luke and Benny." Derek watched him.

"Still... I haven't done *that* in a long time."

Derek tilted his head. "Done what in a long time?"

"Nothing. Nothing." He took a deep breath, shaking it off.

"I don't know, I think you were going to say something that might have surprised me."

"Nah. I just.... It's a new life now."

"You'll have to tell me about your old life sometime." Derek waved at his open jeans. "Should I do up, or can we salvage this if we adjourn to the bedroom or something?"

"I don't have sheets on yet, but...." There was something about Derek that made him need. Despite it being new, despite neighbors peeping in the window, despite everything.

Derek bounced on his heels. "I'll help you put them on."

"Yeah?" How could he resist that enthusiasm? "Come on."

"You don't have to ask me twice." Derek followed him down the hall, almost like an eager puppy.

They walked into the bedroom, and together they moved the dresser against the wall, getting it where Sawyer needed it.

"Making me work for it, eh?" Derek laughed and stole a kiss.

"Now we can get to the bed, at least."

"Oh, you got a king. Good man. Lots of room for everyone." Derek waggled his eyebrows.

"It's nice and sturdy." Places for ties and cuffs too. *Stop it. Stop. It.* He had to let that part of his past go, like he'd let go of the house and the furniture. He was starting new.

"Where's the sheets? I can't wait to pound you into the mattress." There was no waggling of eyebrows this time; Derek looked totally serious.

"I just washed them. They're brand-new." He went to the hall and pulled them out of the little stackable washer and dryer that had come with the apartment, bringing them back into the bedroom in short order.

"I love the smell of clean sheets," Derek told him.

"I do too, and these were a splurge. They're super soft."

Derek took them from him. "Oh wow. Yeah, these are great. It's gonna be amazing rolling around on them."

"It will be, I think. That's why I chose them." Some things were worth spending the extra money on, and sheets were one of those things. Whether he was going to share them or not, they would always be soft and welcoming.

Derek took another kiss. Then they made the bed, working together easily to get the four corners tucked in, then loading the pillows into their cases and spreading the top sheet over the bed. Derek jumped on as soon as the sheets were done, bouncing on Sawyer's brand-new mattress and laughing. "Oh yeah, feels great."

"Does it? Did I choose well?" He sat on the end of the bed, the pillow top supporting him well.

"Yeah, I love it." Derek sat up and pulled Sawyer's shirt off his shoulders. Then Derek snugged up against his back, generating heat between their bodies.

"Oh...." Sawyer's head fell back, and he moaned.

Derek buried his face in the juncture where his neck met his shoulders and placed long openmouthed kisses on his neck. "You taste good."

"Thank you." *Also, don't stop. God.*

Derek slid his hands around Sawyer's waist, warm and tickling softly. The agile fingers went right for the fastenings on his jeans, tugging the button open, then working on the zipper.

His needy cock popped right out, eager for more touches, more caresses. Derek groaned and pushed Sawyer's jeans down before grabbing hold of his cock, wrapping his fingers around it, and squeezing.

"Please," Sawyer whispered. "Don't stop." It was magical—the mouth and the hand and the heat behind him.

"Won't. I want this too." Derek rolled against his ass, cock hard, hot, even through Derek's jeans.

He cried out at the promise there, the sound shocking and loud. Derek moaned around his skin, and he swore he could feel it in his bones. He wanted to feel that sweet prick slamming into him. Making him feel every damn inch inside him.

"You want a twofer, Sawyer?" Derek asked, voice thick. "I'll make you come like this, and then we'll get down to it?"

"Please. Yes. I want it." He might even need it right now. He hadn't known how much he'd been missing this until now, until Derek had woken everything back up in him.

"Yeah, you do." Derek pressed a thumb against his slit, then began a fast stroke, fingers squeezing as they slid up and down his hot flesh.

Sawyer bucked up into the touch, his thighs hard as rocks as he moved. Derek used his free hand to touch Sawyer's pierced nipples, pinching lightly.

Oh, harder, he wished. *Please.*

Then Derek grabbed one of the rings and tugged, still fairly gently. The harder finally came when Derek twisted the metal. Sawyer groaned, bouncing hard on Derek's lap.

"Right. Not just for decoration." Derek played enthusiastically with the little rings, tugging and twisting one, then the other, sending jolts to Sawyer's cock over and over.

"Jesus. Jesus, so good. Please." *Don't stop. God, don't stop.* He thought it might do him in if Derek stopped.

"I love these. And the smooth all over. I told you already how hot that is, right?" Derek sounded half-incoherent, the words barely coming out.

"Uh-huh." He was lost, flying, not worried about anything but his pleasure.

Derek began squeezing the head of his cock hard as he stroked. With every squeeze came a twist to one of the rings on his nipples. The sensations came hard and fast, keeping him writhing. He wanted to shoot, wanted a kiss, wanted a hard, deep fucking. He wanted to be given permission to take his own pleasure from this.

"I want to smell you, Sawyer."

The words, dark and needy and so close to a command, made him arch, spunk spraying from him. Derek moaned, hand working him until the last shudders took him. Then Derek brought his hand up and started licking Sawyer's come from it.

Sawyer whimpered and turned, straddled Derek's hips and brought their lips together. Derek's tongue pushed into his mouth, sharing the taste of his own come with him. He ground them together, rocking good and hard.

"Baby, I want inside you."

"Please. Yes, please." That was exactly what he was craving. He pushed harder, his guiche piercing rubbing so good.

Derek rolled them, pushing him down onto the bed, kissing him with passion. He arched up and took it, opening and allowing himself to let go.

"You got lube?" Derek asked, hand sliding along his side, stopping to tweak his nipple piercing.

"Uh-huh." He did. He'd needed it after this week.

"Where?" Derek backed off, grabbing something out of the pocket of his jeans before shimmying out of them.

He arched over the side of the bed, found the lube, and handed it up. Derek dragged his hand along his body again, fingers warm and firm.

"You should prep yourself," Derek suggested. "I'd love to watch that."

Sawyer flushed, but he knew it was from excitement and anticipation rather than embarrassment. The urge to say "Yes, Sir" was huge, but he simply nodded his agreement and slicked his fingers, eager to feel them inside his ass.

Derek groaned and licked his lips. "God, you're gorgeous."

He turned, showing off, letting Derek see everything. Derek slid his fingers on Sawyer's skin as he moved, touching him like he was precious, special. Like he was needed and necessary.

"Oh yeah, gorgeous."

"Thank you." He spread, encouraging Derek's touch as he slid two fingers into his body and fucked himself with them.

Derek felt him up where his own fingers pushed into his body, and then Derek's long fingers rolled his balls, stroked his cock, tapped his guiche piercing. He moaned, head swaying with his need.

"Okay, I think you're done." Derek's voice was thick, guttural. "I want to fuck you now."

That more than worked for him. "Yes. Yes, please. Now."

Derek helped him get on his hands and knees and settled in behind him. There was the crinkle of the condom, and then he felt Derek's cock at his hole, pressing against him, hot and hard. Derek's hands landed on his asscheeks, thumbs sliding near his crack and spreading him open. Finally, Derek began to push into him.

Sawyer rested his head on his hands, his cock heavy and aching between his thighs. Derek kept moving slowly, pushing and pushing until his cock breached Sawyer's body, then filled it.

Oh yes, that was what he needed. He squeezed hard, saying thank you. Groaning, Derek pulled out nearly all the way, stopping when just the head of his cock was inside Sawyer's body.

"Fuck. Tight. Hot. Good."

"Yeah." That was it, absolutely. So fucking good. Only he needed more, needed Derek pounding into him, not resting there at his entrance, cockhead holding him open.

Groaning, Derek pushed back in, hard and quick, all the way inside him. The head of Derek's cock banged into his gland, lighting up his entire body.

Shit, that was even better than he'd been anticipating.

"More." Oh, he was being bossy, but he couldn't help it. It had been so long, and he needed it so damn badly.

"Needy." Derek made it sound like a compliment. The next thrust inside him felt like one too.

"Yes." He groaned and pulled one leg up under himself, giving Derek more room to take him.

"Fucking love your ass." Derek moved slowly at first, gaining speed as he thrust.

Sawyer couldn't meet each thrust—he wasn't in the right position for that—so he focused on giving Derek something to drive against, on holding himself in place. Derek kept on slamming into him, filling him so good. He took every inch, moaning with it, crying out in his pleasure.

"So hot. So hot. So good." Derek kept repeating the words, semi-incoherent.

"Fuck yes. Take me." He could beg with the best of them.

His words spurred Derek on, the thrusts becoming stronger. The bed was a good one—not a creak or a groan—and he flew, climbing the headboard to push back onto Derek's prick.

Derek sounded like a steam engine behind him, puffing out noisily as Derek worked hard on giving him what he needed. Then Derek shifted and the angle changed, that hard heat knocking up against his gland in the best way.

"Fuck!"

Derek chuckled softly. "There, hmm?"

"Yeah. Right there."

"You got it." Derek dug his fingers harder into Sawyer's hips, pulling him back with every push forward. That sweet cock hit his gland over and over, making him dizzy.

"Fuck. Gonna make me—oh, right there, Derek! Please!" He felt like he was going to shake apart.

Derek didn't touch his cock, but the speed of his thrusts increased, the sound of their flesh slapping together filling the air.

Finally, blessedly, he simply had to give it up and shoot, emptying his balls.

"Oh fuck. Fuck. Fuck." Derek said it each time he jerked into Sawyer before he slammed in one last time and froze.

Sawyer slumped back into Derek's arms, both of them swaying. Derek wrapped his arms around Sawyer and held on to him. "Mmm...."

"Uh-huh." Also whoa and damn.

"Coming out," Derek murmured, putting a hand on the base of his cock, knuckles sliding against Sawyer's ass. "You got a garbage in here?"

"Right over there. The red can."

"Cool." Derek patted his ass and got out of the bed to dump the condom. Then he disappeared into the little en suite, coming out a moment later with a damp cloth, which he used to clean Sawyer.

It was a totally unexpected move.

His cheeks burned, but it felt so intimate, so erotic. Derek tossed the cloth back toward the bathroom, then flopped down next to him. One hand slid along his thigh as Derek gave him a smile. "That was so hot—you're amazing."

"Thank you, for everything." Mostly for insisting. He'd needed that.

Derek stroked his cheek. "My pleasure. Really. You wanna watch a show or something before I help you move furniture around?"

"Sounds great. I'll even buy us supper."

"Yeah? That's terrific. I really like spending time with you."

That was nice to hear. It had been a while. "Thank you."

"You got Netflix? We could find a show we both wanna see but haven't watched yet. Then we've got one we can watch together."

"I do. It's handy, isn't it? Netflix?"

Derek shifted to his side, head on his hand as he gazed at Sawyer. "I love it. And it doesn't matter what kind of show you like, it's there. What kind of show you want to watch?"

"Something easy and fun, huh?"

"We'll have to see if we have the same definition of easy and fun. What about *iZombie*? I've heard good things about that one."

"Sure. I'm willing to try." *iZombie.* Huh.

"Yeah. Zombie girl morgue assistant. Cop. Cute ex-boyfriend and brains. But not in a gross way." Derek found the remote next to the TV and grabbed it, then cuddled in with him again. "You want me to run the remote?"

"Please." He just wanted to float and relax.

Derek soon had it figured out, finding the show and turning on the first episode. Then they settled together as they watched.

It was so... easy. He let himself rest.

The show was amusing, and Derek had a great laugh, chest moving against him.

Derek's phone began to buzz about an hour into their watching, a third of the way through the second episode or so.

Derek leaned over the bed to reach his pants, offering him a great view of a sexy butt and the long line of back. "'Lo? Uh-huh. We're just hanging out."

Oh, did Derek need to go?

"I am not hogging him." Derek leaned down and nuzzled his temple. "Can we invite our evil neighbors for pizza?"

"Uh… sure?" They weren't really evil, peeking through his windows aside.

Derek grinned. "How can I be hogging him if he's buying pizza for all of us?"

Sawyer rolled his eyes and moved to get dressed and put the apartment together.

"I don't know—let's say an hour or so, we're still fixing the furniture. Okay, okay. See you then." Derek hung up and got out of bed too, grabbing his jeans. "So what's first?"

"I'm going to put the living room together. If I have to, I can shut the bedroom door."

"Hey, if it would be easier to have everyone at my place, I don't mind. The guys just want to get to know you, and well, free pizza. I don't think anyone ever said no to that." Derek grinned at him, then stole a quick kiss. "Okay, just tell me where stuff should go, and I'll move it and unpack shit and whatever you need."

"I think I like the sofa against the windows." It was lovely and comfortable—a bright red monstrosity that promised lovely naps. It had certainly done them well earlier until they'd rolled off it.

"You got it." Derek went to the far end and grabbed it from the bottom, then waited patiently for him to grab the other end.

He was pretty sure Derek was doing most of the lifting, because it didn't seem that heavy as they moved it into place by the windows.

It didn't take long before things were in place, and suddenly the house looked like his, like a home almost.

"We've totally got time to fix up your bedroom too, if you want."

"Yeah. The bed's in place there, huh?" And christened too.

"Uh-huh. You need the dresser and that little desk moved around in there?" Derek flexed. "Have muscles, will work."

"Uhn." The sound slipped out of him.

Derek beamed and came over to give him a kiss. "You are damn good for my ego, Sawyer."

"You're a good-looking man."

Tall and tanned, Derek was lanky, with fine muscles. Lord, the man had a beautiful body. And a bright smile with gray eyes that were topped by shaggy blond hair.

"I'm glad you think so, Sawyer, because you're pretty damn hot yourself."

"Thank you. That's good to hear."

Derek leaned in again and raised his head for the kiss that was coming, only to be interrupted by a knock on the door.

Derek rolled his eyes. "That'll be the guys."

"They have timing, huh?" He nodded toward the door. "I'll let you do the honors."

"You sure? It's your place." Derek went to the door, hand on the knob, and waited for his answer.

"Go ahead. They're your friends."

"Soon to be yours too." Derek opened the door, Benny and Luke coming right in and filling the room with testosterone and noise.

They both hugged Derek, then came over.

"Sawyer. We've missed you at the backyard barbeques."

"I've been working." He'd been hiding, but that was his to know.

"Ew." Luke winked and hugged him. "Not working so hard you and Derek couldn't get busy."

"I...." What did he say to that?

Benny elbowed Luke in the side. "He just means that we're jealous Derek's gotten to know you before we did. We're actually a pretty tight little 'friendship.'"

"Yes. I... I walked in on you before." And he needed to remember that. He wasn't special to Derek, any more than Derek was special to him yet. Derek was a free spirit and liked having sex. This was another world.

"Yeah, you should have stayed. We would have shared." Benny's smile was warm. "You've got a powerful need in you."

His cheeks went red-hot, burning down to the bone.

"Hey, there's no reason to be embarrassed." Benny put a hand on his arm. "We're all friends here."

"The place looks great," Luke noted. "And that is a great couch."

Derek caught his gaze and winked.

"Thank you." God, he didn't know where to look.

The guys sat, Luke on the couch, Benny in the recliner. Derek sat on the couch too, and tugged Sawyer down between him and Luke.

"So what's your story?" Benny asked.

"I moved from the West Coast. I'm a copywriter. I have new furniture." *I'm a drunk. My husband died. I used to have a very different life than I do now.*

The three of them looked at him expectantly, like they were waiting for more.

"That's really about it. I'm not exciting."

Luke snorted. "Everyone's got a story. Especially if they pick up and move across the country."

"Maybe he doesn't want to talk about it," Derek suggested.

"After I lost my husband to cancer, I needed a fresh start."

"Oh, of course," Luke offered. "That makes sense."

"Yeah," said Benny.

Derek put his arm around Sawyer's shoulder and squeezed him.

"Thank you. It's been a few years. It was time for a move."

"So we're your new beginning." Luke looked pleased about that.

"Yes. Exactly. I swear to be a good neighbor, though. Seriously."

"I imagine you're already being a good neighbor. Eh, Derek?"

"You're a great neighbor," Derek told him.

"Shh." Oh, he was lit up.

"It's true." Derek dropped his arm behind Sawyer's back, fingers lingering on his ass.

"Oh...," he hummed softly, the praise making him flush.

Derek leaned in slowly and left a soft kiss on his lips.

"So what kind of pizza are we having?" Benny asked, eyes shining.

"What are you guys into?" He liked pepperoni, personally.

Luke opened his mouth, and Benny and Derek said, at the same time, "On your pizza."

Luke pouted.

Sawyer began to laugh—he couldn't help it. They were so charming.

"I like meat," Luke informed him, and that had Benny and Derek laughing as well.

"So, a meat lovers, a pepperoni, and…?"

"I like pineapple and jalapenos," Derek said. "But I'm the only one, so get a small."

Luke and Benny made gagging noises, and Derek flipped them off.

"Don't judge—I like sweet and spicy."

"No judging. Everyone has their thing." Sawyer got that. Derek beamed at him and then dropped him another quick kiss.

"As long as we don't have to eat it." Benny was still making a face.

"I'll go order the pizza. Cokes for everyone?"

There was a chorus of agreement, and Derek gave his back a soft stroke.

"I wouldn't say no to something dessert-like," Luke said. "And I bet I'm not the only one."

"Do you know what my options are? This is my first pizza order here."

"If you call Numoi's—which is right around the corner and frankly the best pizza in town—they've got cheesecake donuts that are very good and then something they call butterscotch tiramisu. And it's to die for."

"You are such a whore for dessert, Benny."

"Who isn't?" Sawyer asked, then went to call for supper—Cokes and pies and desserts and a salad, because green.

When he got back to the living room, Benny was regaling them with a story about working out at the gym and how he almost killed himself on a treadmill with a faulty belt. Luke and Derek were howling with laughter.

He went to sit at the little bar, perching on a barstool and admiring the little tableau. Both Benny and Luke were bigger than Derek, more muscled. One blond, the other brunet. They were both studs. Honestly, all three of them were.

He was smaller, leaner, but there was a fineness to that too.

Derek glanced over at him and smiled. Then he held out a hand, inviting him back to the couch.

Sawyer headed over, that hand irresistible. Derek made room between him and Benny, and when he sat, Benny gave him a soft smile too.

It was warm between them, heat pouring from their bodies and seeping into him.

"That's a gorgeous sight," Luke hummed.

Funny, he'd been thinking the same thing about them.

"Yeah, Sawyer fits well, doesn't he?" Derek patted his thigh.

"Yeah, he does. You guys make a sexy, sexy picture altogether."

"Do we?" Benny looked at him and Derek, then reached out for him. His eyes went wide as Benny cupped his cheek. "You're warm."

"Th-thank you." What was this? He didn't do this. Share. Did he?

Benny leaned in and pressed their lips together. "Mmm. You taste good."

He gasped, his heart slamming. "Is this—this is unusual for me."

Derek slid his hand along Sawyer's back. "Unusual is not necessarily a bad thing, is it? I mean, if you don't want this, we'll just have pizza."

"But we'd rather have pizza and you," Benny told him before taking another soft, light kiss.

What would James think?

Hell, James would sit back in that recliner, thighs parted, and watch.

Suddenly he missed James so much it physically hurt, and he grabbed for Benny, for comfort. Groaning, Benny wrapped an arm around him and parted his lips, tongue pushing in.

"That's it, Sawyer. We have you." Derek's voice was low, excited.

Benny kept kissing him, tongue filling his mouth, exploring him. The hand cradling his cheek tilted his head slightly, and the kiss went deeper still. Benny eased him back against Derek, giving him the muscled chest to rest against.

Derek slid his hands around Sawyer's waist and brought them to rest on his hips, fingers framing his cock. It jerked, trying to fill.

Derek hummed and kissed his neck, lips warm and soft. "You're okay. We're okay."

Was he? He thought maybe he was. Or okay enough that he could enjoy this.

Benny's kisses became firmer, and Derek's became wet and sucking, maybe even leaving marks on his body.

Luke moaned from across the coffee table, the sound deep and wanton. "I want to see his cock, boys. Show him off for me."

Derek was the one who popped the top button of his jeans, but it was Benny who slowly drew his zipper down.

"You're going to love this," Derek moaned.

"Ink?"

"Metal, and he's bare."

"You shave?" Benny asked. "God, I could so shave you."

Derek shook his head. "It's permanent."

Both Benny and Luke moaned loudly.

"Were you lifestyle, Sawyer? Twenty-four/seven?"

Sawyer nodded once, answering Luke.

Derek gasped softly and grabbed his hips, fingers opening and closing.

"Fuck yes." Benny tugged Sawyer's pants and underwear down, and his cock sprang out eagerly without him even meaning for it to happen. "Look at you. So pretty. Luke, can you see?"

"Take his jeans right off and spread him so I can see properly." Luke's voice was deep, growly, full of need.

Derek moaned again, and between him and Benny, they soon had Sawyer naked—pants, underwear, and shirt tossed aside, leaving him bare, exposed.

"The pizza guy will come...." Not that his cock cared. He didn't either, actually. At all.

"I'll take care of it, Sawyer. You don't have to worry about a thing." Luke's voice was low, seductive.

"I don't...." But he did, and he relaxed back into Derek, spread wide.

Derek moaned again, fingers sliding over his skin. They left tingles behind, tingles that were intensified by Luke's gaze. "So good, honey. I fucked him, Luke, and he took me like a dream."

They all moaned at that, him included.

"You like him, Derek, hmm?"

"Fuck yes."

Pleased, Sawyer kissed the side of his face.

Benny ran one hand up his leg, sliding along his skin.

He felt exposed and open and so alive for the first time in a lot of years.

"Look at you, blooming with touch."

Luke's words should have made him squirm, but instead they made him arch and beg silently for more. It was like Luke knew exactly what buttons to push and how to push them, rusty as they were.

God, they must think he was such a needy slut. Truth was—that he was.

Benny's mouth headed south. Derek took the opportunity and tilted his head to the side so Derek could kiss him. This kiss was deep and wild, heady, stealing his breath.

Shifting behind him, Derek slid a hard, jeans-clad cock against his spine. That sensation drowned in the lightning that shot through him when Benny wrapped his mouth around Sawyer's right nipple, tongue working the ring.

Then Derek grabbed Benny's hand and brought it between Sawyer's legs to the guiche hidden there. Benny's happy gasp blew cold air around his nipple, making it tighten, but it was the way Benny twisted the guiche that made *him* gasp.

His toes curled, and he pushed a cry into Derek's lips. His cock jerked, and he arched slightly, wanting a touch, needing it. He would have begged, but Derek still had his mouth occupied.

Benny pinched and tugged, working his nipples, his rings. It was so much better than his own hands. So much more, so much bigger.

He didn't know what to do, so he went with his training and relaxed, melting and opening.

"You've been taught well," murmured Luke.

Oh, that was so good to hear: that even now, he honored his Dom.

"One of you touch the poor man's cock."

Immediately, two different hands slid along his prick, one larger than the other and rougher.

His abs clenched, and he cried out, the urge to shoot fierce.

"Don't come yet, boy. This is our first chance to play with you, and we want it to last."

He looked to Derek, begging. Derek met his gaze and smiled, took his mouth again. Wrapping a hand around his cock, Derek began to stroke him.

Oh, Derek learned him so fast. So fast.

"You're still not allowed to come yet," Luke told him.

Benny tugged his balls, pulling steadily, and an ache grew in the pit of his belly. They were building a powerful need in him— all three of them. He reached up, linked his arms around Derek's shoulders.

"Hey, gorgeous." Derek dropped a kiss on his forehead, then another on his nose and another on his chin.

"Hey. This is... wild." He let his eyes close.

"You're wild," whispered Derek. "Wild and gorgeous."

He moaned and arched, bringing their mouths together. Derek's tongue pushed in between his lips, plundering his mouth, and the hand around his cock sped, Derek jacking him fast now.

"Hogging him," Benny complained.

Derek didn't stop kissing him to reply.

Sawyer flew, his body alight and burning with need. Derek and Benny kept him flying, working his nipples and cock, touching him all over.

About the time he was ready to blow, there was a knock on his apartment door, and he cried out in protest.

"I've got it," growled Luke and tossed a T-shirt across Sawyer's groin.

"Be so quiet, little mouse," Benny whispered. "So quiet for us."

He nodded, still caught up in Derek's kisses. He could do quiet. Silent even. The only noise was the sound of their breaths every time their lips parted and they drew in air.

Derek's hand covered his left nipple, Benny's mouth his right.

Then the door shut, and Luke put the food on the pass-through before sitting back down in the recliner. "Keep going, boys. We'll let Sawyer come before we have pizza." Luke grinned. "He's stunning."

Sawyer thought he was more desperate than stunning.

Derek's hand moved faster on his cock, and Benny wrapped his bigger hand around Derek's even as he sucked on Sawyer's nipple, his tongue playing with the ring.

He wrenched his lips from Derek's. "Please!" He couldn't hold on.

"It's up to Luke," Derek whispered. "Luke, he needs to come."

"You can make him come. But then you don't get to. Not this time, anyway."

Derek didn't even pause but kept jacking him, fingers rubbing across the head of his cock, the little burn perfect. "Will you get a ring here, Sawyer? Will you let us watch?"

Benny bit his nipple, and Sawyer's eyes crossed as he shot, his balls emptying.

Derek moaned and kissed him again, sucking on his tongue. The stroking continued, pulling out several aftershocks, some more spunk slipping from him.

"Very nice." Luke's voice was husky, rough, and Sawyer hid in the curve of Derek's jaw.

Benny placed a kiss on his nipple and got up.

Derek hummed and held him, pressing kisses on his head. "He's right. So hot."

Then his robe, soft and warm, covered him. Benny grinned at him. "Was on the back of the door in your bathroom."

"Thank you." Oh God.

Derek helped him get the robe on, then tugged him close, cuddling up with him. "Pizza smells great, doesn't it?"

"Yes." He was trembling hard enough that he didn't know whether he could eat.

Derek hugged him tight, hands sliding up and down his arms. "You're okay."

"I didn't expect this, but yes. I'm okay."

"You're so hot. That was beautiful." Derek continued to cuddle him, warm and good against him.

It was Benny who grabbed the pizza and doled it out, making a face as he gave Derek the pineapple-jalapeno one.

"Shut up, butthead. It's good." Derek stuck his tongue out.

Benny grabbed it with his fingers, then leaned in and gave Derek a hard kiss. Derek groaned and pushed up, giving as good as he got. Now *that* was stunning.

Benny finally backed off, sat next to them, and took a bite out of his meat lovers.

"You want a taste of mine?" Derek asked.

"Sure." He was notoriously not picky. His Dom had ordered for him for years.

Derek held the slice up to his lips, one bite already missing from it. It was sweet and spicy; not what he was used to, but nothing worth gagging over.

"It's good, isn't it?" Derek asked, giving him a hopeful and expectant look.

"It is. I probably wouldn't order it on my own, but I can totally eat it."

Derek beamed at him, then stuck his tongue out at Benny again, who was too far away this time to play.

Luke hadn't said anything either, in favor of scarfing down several pieces of pizza.

"Did you know there's something moldy in one of those containers?" Benny asked.

"Moldy?" Derek asked, frowning.

"Do I need to call the pizza place?"

Luke got up, snorted, and came back with a large container. He set it on the coffee table and opened it. "Salad."

"Salad is good. I love veggies."

"I like salads with good dressings," Derek said.

"Benny's into meat, meat, and more meat," Luke noted.

"I can tell. Those muscles need protein."

"I also like the other meat." Benny waggled his eyebrows and leered, leaving no doubt as to what he meant.

Luke tossed a pillow at him, and Derek laughed. Sawyer curled his legs under him, chuckling softly. It was so good to be among friends. Derek gave him a hug and a smile, eyes bright and happy.

He was pretty sure that moving here had been the best decision he'd made in the last six years.

CHAPTER FOUR

PIZZA AND dessert rocked. Benny ignored the mold, aka the salad. But what really set the evening up was finally getting to spend some quality time with the new neighbor. He was pretty sure Sawyer had been avoiding them ever since the barbecue the first night he popped in. And for a while Benny had wondered if the new guy was going to really fit in. Luke had told him not to stress it, and he hadn't really been stressing, But it was good to know the guy wasn't going to move out in a snit because they all fucked around together.

Now he was fed and happy. They'd gotten Sawyer off before dinner, so now it was his turn. Because Luke had said Derek would have to wait if Sawyer came.

He looked expectantly at Luke once they'd cleared everything away.

Luke raised a single eyebrow. "What?"

"Can the new guy suck me off?" He figured he'd start out like he could hold out.

"You can't take a blow job without coming, so no."

"But I've been good!" Oh, no fair.

"Sawyer got to come, so you and Derek can wait until later in the evening." Luke turned to Sawyer. "If you had carte blanche, what would you want to do right now?"

"Get to know you."

Oh, Sawyer was too sweet.

Benny sighed as Luke beamed at Sawyer. They were going to go with get to know you instead of suck off Benny. He didn't approve.

"Let's play two truths and a lie," Luke suggested.

"Ooh. I like that game." Benny bounced and grabbed another piece of pizza.

"Then you can start," Luke told him.

"I love to fuck. I love to be fucked. I'm a virgin."

Everyone laughed, and Derek shouted out, "The virgin thing is a lie! Are we getting prizes?"

Benny swung his gaze around to Luke, who twisted his lips and *hmm*ed. "He who figures out the most lies gets to come next."

"So I have one. I'm ahead!" Derek hooted and danced, making Sawyer laugh. Derek winked at Sawyer and sat next to him.

"It's your turn now, though," Luke said. "If you guess right, you have to do it."

"Okay." Derek narrowed his eyes.

"You're thinking hard—I can smell the smoke," Benny noted.

Derek stuck his tongue out. "Benny's a turd, I love my job, and I love tiger tail ice cream more than anything."

"The lie is obviously the first one," Benny said.

"Nope—God's honest truth, that one. But you've narrowed it down for Luke and Sawyer."

"I don't know what tiger tail ice cream is, but it must be good." Sawyer laughed.

"Nope. He hates it. I didn't know that, but I know he loves his job more than is natural." Luke made a tick in the air with his finger. "That's one for me."

"It's not unnatural to love your job. You guys are just jealous. And tiger tail ice cream has a thread of licorice flavoring through it. And not just a little thread either. Talk about unnatural." Derek shook himself. "Yuck."

"No licorice for you. Got it." Sawyer nodded like he'd remember it. Benny bet Sawyer would. There was something about the guy that screamed "I pay attention."

Just like the guy had triggered every one of Luke's big bad top instincts.

"That means you go next, Luke."

"I'm a huge kale fan, I was a go-go dancer in university, and my favorite movie is *Jurassic Park*."

His and Derek's mouths both dropped open. He knew damn well Luke drank lots of kale smoothies; he hated the stuff if it wasn't disguised and deeply hidden.

"You were a go-go dancer?" Derek asked before Benny had a chance to.

Luke's smile was slow and easy, like a crocodile's.

"Why was that the go-to as a truth?" Sawyer asked.

"Because anyone who knows Luke for more than six hours knows he's a huge *Jurassic Park* fan and thinks kale is a necessary evil, which leaves the go-go thing. So who do we have to blow to see a demonstration?"

"I'm older now, broader. There will be no demonstration."

Now that was no fair. No fair at all.

"You work out a ton and your body is amazing," Derek pointed out.

"Go-go dancing is a slender man's game. It's not happening, and if you ask me to demonstrate again, there will be spankings. For everyone."

Sawyer blushed dark, but Benny noticed there didn't seem to be any shock there. Nor any great worry about the possibility of getting spanked either. Benny didn't like it, but Derek got off on it. And on watching him take a spanking from Luke if he'd earned it.

"So who got that one right?" Benny asked.

"Let's give Sawyer a turn. He hasn't yet, and he knows us the least, so he's got less of a chance of answering as quickly as you two hooligans."

Benny had to admit he was interested in what Sawyer's truths were. They didn't know a whole lot about him yet, but he seemed onionlike. Lots of layers.

"Oh, I... I write copy for catalogs, I published a horror novel years ago, and I, um, don't know how to knit."

"No way you published a horror novel," exclaimed Benny.

"I don't know," said Derek. "I think it'd be way more interesting if that was true and the lie is that you don't know how to knit. Because that would mean you do know how to knit, and that would be kind of funky and cool."

Sawyer nodded. "Derek got it. I can totally knit."

Derek laughed softly and planted a kiss on his lips.

Benny frowned. "No way. Seriously? And did you already know, Derek? 'Cause I think you're cheating."

"He didn't tell me. Like I said, it seemed funky and cool. And dude—you published a horror novel?"

Sawyer pinked. "I did. I'm almost done with another. It was on hold while James was sick."

"That's so cool! Well, not that James was sick, but the whole published horror novel that you wrote and you're writing another one."

Okay, Derek was stupid in lust with Sawyer; that much was clear to Benny. It was adorable, really. Like truly cute.

"It's your turn again, Derek," Luke prompted.

"Okay, let's see, I don't want to make it so easy this time...." Derek got a faraway look for a moment, and then he went on. "I'm one class short of graduating high school. My first time was with one of my teachers in the school parking lot. And I've always wanted a ferret."

"A teacher? Impressive. Man or woman?" Benny asked. Derek was just a baby.

"Dude, I was never into women. So you figured that one was true. Which of the other two is a lie?" Derek looked around the room expectantly, eyes lingering on Sawyer.

"Ferrets are cool." Sawyer twined their fingers together.

"They smell, though." Derek laughed softly. "I don't really want one. Though a rabbit would be nice, don't you think?"

"Are we allowed pets?" Sawyer asked. "I like cats."

"Nobody ever said we couldn't have them. You think a bunny and a cat would get along?"

"I don't know." Sawyer moved to push into his arms, stealing a kiss.

"No fair!"

"Benny." Luke growled out his name.

"Well, it's not."

"I didn't say no kissing...."

In that case.... He pushed into Luke's arms and smashed their lips together. Luke wrapped around him and brought him in, taking over control of the kiss immediately. Benny didn't roll over and beg for more, but he did let Luke have his head. Luke could do anything he wanted to Benny.

Hell, Luke could do anything he wanted to any of them, he'd bet.

The kiss ended far sooner than he wanted, and he pouted.

"God, you're a brat." Luke was smiling as he said it.

"You know it. Your brat."

Luke wrapped a hand around the back of his neck and pulled him in for another no-holds-barred kiss that he felt down to his bones. Fuck, that was something else. Benny melted, hand cupping Luke's cheek. God, he loved this man. Drawing circles on the small of his back with his fingers, Luke held him. He hummed for Benny before breaking the kiss again. "You can do what you want with him, Derek, but don't forget you're not allowed to come yet."

"I know. He's just so fucking sweet."

"Baby boy's got it bad for the new guy," Benny murmured, looking back at them again.

"Uh-huh. Can't say I blame him."

"He's not bad at all." Benny shook his head, but you couldn't be growly at Sawyer. The man was nice as hell.

Luke's hand slid to his ass, grabbed a cheek, and squeezed. "Damning with faint praise." Luke watched Derek and Sawyer, then turned his gaze back to Benny. "Remember, you're not allowed to come yet either."

"I'm not stupid, Luke. I heard you. I won't forget."

"I didn't say you were stupid, boy." Oh, he did love it when Luke growled. Even when it was at him.

"I'm not forgetful either." He cuddled in.

"So, are we done playing?" Luke asked loudly enough the other two could hear him.

"If we quit now, I win," Derek pointed out.

"I think that's cheating." Benny thought about it a moment longer. "No, I know that's cheating."

Luke shrugged. "We're making up our own rules."

"Who won the last round?" he asked.

"Uh...." Luke chuckled. "I'm a little distracted. Who gave the last truths and lie?"

Derek waved from his kiss.

"I don't think anyone guessed that right. We all assumed it was the high school thing. You really didn't graduate?"

"Nope."

"Wow." Benny couldn't imagine, but it didn't seem to matter, did it?

Derek shrugged. "It's not like I needed my high school degree to work at the family factory."

"True," Sawyer added. "True, and what you do is a special skill."

Derek beamed at Sawyer. "Thank you."

"Good lord, would you two just fuck already?"

"Too late, Benny, they already have."

Sawyer looked over with a hurt expression. Then he backed away from Derek. "I'm going to get some clothes on. I'll be right back."

Then Sawyer was gone, and the bedroom door shut and locked with a loud click.

Derek glared at him and Luke. "What the hell was that?"

"We were just teasing."

"Guys, he's new and obviously delicate! Way more than us." Derek got up and went over to the bedroom door. "Sawyer? It's me. Open the door?"

Benny sighed. "Was I an asshole? I didn't mean to be an asshole."

"No. He's just scared, I bet. He doesn't know where to settle yet, what's a joke and what's criticism."

"The kid's pissed off at us."

"Uh-huh. He'll come back around too."

"Please, Sawyer? The guys are going to clean up and leave." Derek gave them a glare that said they'd better do that.

"Oh, I'm okay. I just felt odd being the only one in a robe." Sawyer appeared, wearing sweats and a loose T-shirt. "Should I grab the dessert?"

"Yeah? You sure you're okay?" Derek asked, stroking Sawyer's arm.

"I am. I just needed a little armor, hmm?"

Derek nodded, and the two of them came back to the couch and sat together.

"So we're all good again?" Luke asked.

"Sorry, Sawyer. I was just teasing, not trying to hurt your feelings, man," Benny said. See him. See him be nice.

Luke nodded and slid a hand along his back.

"I'll learn," Sawyer said. "I know I'm stupidly sensitive. I'm trying not to be, but... it's hard."

"Have you always been that way?" Luke asked. "I mean, was that your demeanor during your time together?"

"Me and my... James?"

"Yes, that's what I meant." Luke gave Sawyer a sympathetic look but continued to hold his gaze.

"He was my professor. I think he knew that I was... less than confident. After he died, I was lost, and I drank, a lot. Now I'm sober and single and less than confident again."

Poor man. God, Benny couldn't imagine losing Luke or Derek, either one.

"That really sucks. I'm sorry. The information is important to know, though."

Derek held Sawyer, kissed his cheek. "You're okay now. You're with friends."

It really was cute the way Derek had it so bad for Sawyer.

Benny relaxed back against Luke.

"What kind of professor?" Luke asked.

"English. He was brilliant."

"I bet he was. And he took good care of you." Luke's tone was easy and light.

"He did, but I took care of him as well. It was a mutually beneficial love affair."

"That's great. I can see why it was so hard to lose him. It's good you're moving on now, though."

"You can't just wait forever for him to not be dead, I guess," Benny added.

Sawyer looked over at him, then blinked. "You know what, you're absolutely right. After almost five years, he's probably... gooey."

"Ewww." Derek made a face. "I really don't want to be imagining what I'm imagining right now."

"No, me either." Sawyer grinned, though, and the look was surprisingly wicked.

Benny had to laugh. And the others joined in. Okay, he thought he could get to enjoy Sawyer's company a lot. The guy just might fit in with them. He was absolutely trying, and Benny could respect that.

"Soooo." He looked at Luke. "We were promised someone would get to orgasm…." And he very much wanted it to be him.

Luke nodded. "I did say that, didn't I?" The long legs spread. "Come and give me my orgasm."

"Oh, that's totally cheating!" Benny pinched the inside of Luke's thigh, careful not to hurt.

"No, baby, that's the perks to being the one in charge."

"Is it? Why did I pick being a sub again?"

"You didn't pick it, baby. It picked you. *I* picked you."

Derek hummed cheerfully. "You two make me happy."

Benny stole a kiss, slow and lazy, while working Luke's belt open.

"Can Sawyer blow me while Benny's blowing you, Luke?" Derek asked.

"Is that fair?" Benny whispered against Luke's lips.

"You just want to come too."

Well, duh.

Luke chuckled. "Go ahead, Sawyer. Blow Derek's mind."

"It's not his mind he wants blown," Benny noted.

"I'd be happy to." Sawyer slid down, kissing Derek's chest on the way.

"I want a kiss first," Derek murmured, bending to bring their mouths together.

Benny shook his head. It really wasn't fair, but at the same time, he wasn't giving up his chance to suck Luke's amazing cock.

"Shh. You know I have your back, baby."

"I know."

"Show me how much you love my cock, and then I'll return the favor."

Benny moved down between Luke's legs, sliding down Luke's fly. The first thing that hit him was the scent of Luke's cock. The second he smelled it, his own cock perked up.

He nuzzled in and fished Luke out, careful not to catch Luke on his zipper. That earned him a low moan, and Luke spread his legs farther apart, giving him more room to work.

"Smell so good." Luke made him a little dizzy, if he was honest.

"I'm leaking for you, baby. Every last drop is yours."

He whimpered, so pleased he burned. He dragged his tongue from the base to the tip of that fat, thick prick. Fuck, he loved this cock. Loved Luke.

Luke dropped a hand onto his head, solid and warm but not forcing him in any way.

It was so easy to sink into this, to moan and lick and let himself lean close. Luke began to pet him, fingers stroking through his hair and sliding down to caress his jaw, his throat.

God, so good. So hot and right. He began to suck, pulling strong but slow. Luke moaned for him, the sound sexy as hell and going straight to his balls.

An answering sound came from Derek, a little wilder, a little louder. Benny redoubled his efforts—he could make Luke need harder than Sawyer could work Derek.

"Damn, baby." Luke shifted, pushing closer.

He'd have smiled, but his mouth was a little busy and very full. He slapped the tip of Luke's cock with his tongue as he pulled up along the hot flesh.

A spurt of salty seed teased his lips. Oh, excellent. He sucked it in, swallowing over and over, loving that flavor.

"Ben. Baby. Fuck...." Luke grabbed his head and began humping up toward his mouth.

Opening up, he let Luke in, swallowing around the thick heat whenever it hit his throat. Luke knew he could take every inch, suck good and hard.

Luke dropped both hands to his head, holding him in place as he fucked Benny's mouth in earnest. That was what he needed, what he wanted, down to the bone.

"Baby. Baby." Luke repeated the word over and over.

He swallowed hard, thumbs working Luke's balls.

"Baby!" This time the endearment was a shout and his only warning as Luke shot and come spurted down his throat.

He took every drop, humming over the flavor. This was his lover, his man.

Luke relaxed back in his chair, one hand remaining in Benny's hair. He cleaned Luke's cock, licking gently.

He could hear Derek and Sawyer kissing slowly. He was patient, though, cleaning every single inch before raising his head and begging his own kiss.

"So good," Luke murmured, drawing him up.

Big as he was, he loved that it didn't feel awkward for him to be in Luke's lap. He shared one kiss after another, offering Luke a taste of himself.

Luke's hands were so warm, holding him easily.

"So when do I get to come?" He tried not to sound whiny.

"You have been patient, haven't you?"

He nodded. He so had. Patient as anyone. And everyone else had gotten to come already.

"All right, get up and get naked. Then you can come sit here again, and Derek and Sawyer can blow you."

He nodded eagerly, standing up to strip, tear off his clothes.

Luke chuckled softly. "That is some very eager stripping." Then Luke turned to the others. "Poor Benny hadn't gotten to come yet. You two want to come help him out with that?"

"Uh-huh." Derek turned to Sawyer. "Benny's got a great cock, and he tastes good."

"He's been very kind and patient, at least so far." Luke pulled him down and hooked Benny's legs around his, which held Benny open.

"That is very unusual," Derek noted.

"Hey!" Benny argued. "I'm patient!"

"When it comes to sex?" Derek shook his head, and Luke chuckled behind him, jiggling him somewhat.

Derek and Sawyer came over and knelt together in front of him.

Sawyer's hands were soft on his legs, while Derek was more straightforward, mouth dropping down on his prick. The suction made his eyes cross, made him cry out.

"Don't be greedy, Derek," Luke warned. "Besides, I want you to take your time, play with him. Make Benny wait for it."

That was his wicked lover.

"So mean to me," he groused.

"I could show you mean," Luke warned. "I'm sure Derek and Sawyer could just as happily suck each other off while we watch."

He didn't think either one of them could get it up again, personally.

"I'm happy sucking Benny," Derek said. "He deserves his turn."

"You are too sweet, Derek." Luke patted Benny's hip. "I shall have to come up with the appropriate punishment for sassing me. I have yet to find it."

Sawyer licked and stroked, the tiniest caresses making Benny dizzy. And distracting him from what Luke was saying. Meanwhile, Derek had found his balls, sucking first one in and then the other.

Sawyer licked the tip of his cock, the motion unbearably gentle. He shook, his body vibrating from it.

Luke hummed. "He likes that, boys. Whatever you're doing is driving him crazy."

"Uh-huh. Nuts. So good. Please."

"You heard him, Derek. He wants more action on his nuts."

At Luke's words, Derek sucked harder on Benny's balls. Benny moaned softly in thanks, his sac wrinkling up.

Derek was like a hoover and Sawyer like a feather, the contrasting touches maddening in the best way. He shifted in Luke's lap, his entire body lit up.

Luke pushed a hand between his body and Benny's ass, one finger sliding along his crack toward his hole.

"Please. Please, Luke." He wanted it.

"Please what, boy? This?" Luke pushed his finger against Benny's hole, pressing hard, then breaching him.

"Yes!" He shuddered, not sure where to put his body.

"I love the way your body shakes when you don't know whether to push forward or press back." Luke nibbled on his neck, finger pressing in again and again.

"I can't help it. Love. More, please. Please, Sawyer. Derek."

Luke nodded. "Give him more. He begs so prettily for it."

Sawyer began to suck him, and his eyes went wide. Fuck. The man was born to this. Sawyer's head began to bob, each slide of the tight lips along Benny's prick like magic.

"Luke!" He needed his lover to know this, how good it was.

"Right here, baby." Luke pushed his finger deeper, the burn the perfect accompaniment to Sawyer's mouth.

"You're going to love this." He bore down.

"I do love fingerfucking you, baby." Luke sent his finger deeper.

"Yes." Hell yeah. He leaned forward, then back.

They worked him together, their mouths and Luke's finger pushing him higher every moment.

"Soon," he whispered. "I can't hold it, Luke."

"Of course you can't. The question is, am I going to make you try?" Luke rubbed their cheeks together.

"Love...." Oh, he was happy, all the way.

"Mmm. I do love you. But I'm going to punish you if you don't wait until I tell you that you can come. I'm going to bind your cock and balls and leave them like that overnight."

"Luke!" Bastard. Luke knew if he kept talking....

"Just laying it out on the line for you. It wouldn't be fair if you came and then I told you that it wasn't allowed and I was going to bind your sac and hang weights from it." Luke nuzzled his temple. "I might even have to plug your ass with something heavy. Leave it in for our workout tomorrow."

He was going to scream.

Sawyer's long moan vibrated around his cock.

"Oh, are you into ass play, Sawyer? Do you need to be plugged and fucked and filled?" Luke was evil incarnate.

This time Sawyer's sound was a whimper, and the suction around Benny's cock increased. Oh, they were going to have so much fun together.

"He loves that idea, Luke," he managed to grind out.

"Excellent." Luke bit his earlobe, hard.

He jerked and shot, his spunk pouring into Sawyer. Oh fuck.

"Naughty, naughty, Benny."

He couldn't be sorry. It had been good. Like fucking good. "If you knew what Sawyer was like, you'd totally understand." He looked down at the man who was cleaning him, licking him like his cock was a lollipop. "You are something else."

Sawyer turned bright red, but the licking didn't stop. Someone was a bigger cockhound than Benny, and that was saying a lot.

He reached down and stroked Sawyer's hair. "Thank you."

"What am I? Shoe scum?" Derek asked. "My mouth was there too."

"I can't reach you, shoe-scum boy."

Derek stuck his tongue out. "Butthead."

Sawyer began to giggle. Derek turned and smiled at Sawyer. "Dude, I still think that's the best sound."

"Thank you." Sawyer leaned forward and kissed Derek gently.

Derek closed his eyes and kissed Sawyer back. If they weren't so pretty together, Benny probably would have said something sarcastic, but they were, and so he didn't. Instead he rested back against Luke, coming down slowly. The anticipation of his "punishment" kept his tension at a certain level.

It felt good, to relax, to be together. He'd worried about the new guy. But he seemed to not only be fitting in okay, but fitting in well. It seemed he was less vanilla than he looked.

Like a metric fuckton less.

"So tell us, Sawyer. You have a king-size bed, right?" Luke asked.

"I do, yes. I just bought it. It's brand-new."

"Good man. There's way more room for four in a king."

"Let me show you my bedroom."

"Perfect." Luke stretched, and Benny slid from his lover's lap, Derek and Sawyer standing in front of them.

The big bed was already mussed, but there were plenty of pillows and heavy comforters. Someone got cold.

"This'll do nicely. Who wants to be the middle?" Luke asked.

"Sawyer, I think." Benny grinned at his new friend, then climbed in and held one hand out for Sawyer.

"I'll take the other middle." Derek was so in lust.

Luke chuckled. "I haven't cuddled you in an age, Derek."

"I know. Slacker," Derek teased.

Luke grabbed Derek around the neck and gave him a noogie. They bumped into Sawyer, sending the man onto the bed and into Benny's arms.

He wrapped his arms around Sawyer, hugged him. "Hey."

"Hey there."

Derek snuggled up behind Sawyer, and Luke got in after him, bumping them all toward Benny, pushing Sawyer more firmly into his arms.

"Perfect. Everyone can rest now." Luke sounded so sure.

"Yes, Mr. Bossy." Derek gave Benny a grin.

Benny grinned back. Hopefully Luke's hands weren't too full.

CHAPTER FIVE

LUKE LIKED the new guy. He'd clearly come from a background in the lifestyle. He'd have to gently grill him, find out where his limits were, what he was into. Aside from oral. And anal. He grinned up at the ceiling. It seemed that under the quiet exterior, Sawyer was as sexual as the rest of them.

He was pretty, gentle, obviously smart, and a touch skittish, but he seemed to be willing to try, to meet them all halfway. And that was a big ask of someone new—taking on three guys who had been playing together for ages.

He glanced at the time. Well after midnight. No wonder he was feeling like he needed a snack. Luke slipped out of bed and padded out to Sawyer's kitchen to see if he stocked decent snacks in either his pantry or his fridge.

There were grapes and turnovers, apples and lunch meat. All good stuff.

"Feel free to help yourself." The soft sound made him jump.

"Hey, Sawyer. I didn't realize anyone else was awake." He held out his arms. Would Sawyer take him up on his invitation?

"I felt you get up. I'm a light sleeper." Sawyer stepped closer, coming to him.

He wrapped Sawyer in a hug, offering him warmth, comfort. "Is that something you learned so you would always be there for your master?"

"It was what I did for him, to make sure he had what he needed."

"You were twenty-four/seven in it, eh?" That must have made the loss even harder.

"Yes, Sir. I was."

Sweet boy.

"Well, you're a credit to him, from what I've seen."

"I have had a few hard years, but I brought myself back from the edge."

"The alcoholism." He nodded. He'd bet Sawyer had been unbelievably lost after he'd lost his master.

"Yes. I didn't... I'm not proud of it, but it happened."

"But you turned your life back around. Well done. Now, what shall we snack on?"

"Would you like a sandwich?"

"Actually, yes, I would. Thank you." He could have made it himself, but he had a hunch that Sawyer would appreciate the role of caretaker.

"I have turkey and ham, cheddar or provolone."

"Turkey and provolone, please. And I hope you'll join me."

"Do you like any dressing? Veg? Do you prefer toasted?"

"Make it how you like it." He leaned back against the counter, watching Sawyer move. Graceful. The man was graceful.

Sawyer put a pan on the stove, then began to build sandwiches—turkey and cheese and a bit of tomato, then toasted with a little pot of aioli to dip in.

It made him think that Sawyer was maybe pleased that his neighbors had suddenly turned into a top and a pair of brats who all loved sex and were more than happy to pull him in. Some men found peace in being a sub. Not just in the sexual aspect, but in every aspect.

"This looks amazing."

"Thank you. What would you like to drink?"

"What have you got, boy?"

"Milk, soda, orange juice, and water."

"Better make it water because soda'll mean I won't get back to sleep. Once you have everything, come sit with me."

"Yes, Sir." Sawyer made another sandwich for himself and grabbed two bottles of water before coming over to Luke.

He pushed away from the table and patted his leg. He wanted Sawyer on his lap.

"Oh...." Sawyer came to him, swallowing hard.

He stroked Sawyer's cheek with the back of his hand. "You okay, boy?"

"Yes. Yes, I... I love to sit with a strong man."

Smiling, Luke slid his arm around Sawyer as he sat. He fit perfectly.

"Eat your sandwich, sweet boy." He stroked Sawyer's back in slow, easy lines.

He dipped his own, loving the crunchiness of the fried bread. Damn, he hadn't had an amazing midnight snack like this in forever. He was thinking they would keep Sawyer.

He loved Benny and Derek, but Sawyer would be a new dynamic, someone with an entirely new experience. And he thought maybe Sawyer needed him in a way the other two didn't. Not more or anything, but differently.

"This really is good. I'm feeling spoiled."

"I'm glad you like it. Cooking wasn't a natural talent, but I learned to love it."

"You find it hard cooking for one?" It was one of the reasons they'd first come together. Who wanted to grill burgers for one?

"I hate it."

"Does that mean that if we all share groceries, you'd cook in exchange for things we can do for you? And I don't mean that sexually. I mean, Benny's great with household repairs, and Derek keeps us in all the ice cream we want and always has the latest games on his system. Things like that."

"I can, yes. I enjoy it. It's relaxing, you know?"

"Well, I burn everything I put anywhere near the stove, so I don't know from personal experience, but I can understand in theory how it could be relaxing." Grinning, he took another bite of his sandwich. "Definitely going to get spoiled if this sandwich is anything to go by."

Sawyer leaned in, resting against him, watching him eat. He kept his hand moving slowly over Sawyer's back. His gut was telling him that Sawyer craved the contact.

"This is okay with your boy? With Derek?"

"If it hadn't been, we wouldn't have played with you earlier. I can tell you a secret. We were hoping you'd be willing to play with us."

"Were you? Did you with the person that was here before?"

"No, unfortunately he was very prim and very proper, and he thought that both Benny and Derek were childish and not worthy of his time. I took umbrage at that, and any hint of friendship that might have existed between us and him disappeared."

"Oh…." Sawyer frowned. "Derek has been so kind, and Benny too. He teases, but I know that now."

"They're good men. Both of them. I'm glad you can see that." It made him like Sawyer even more.

"I know I'm sensitive. My master always said my feelings could be hurt in a second."

He kissed the top of Sawyer's head. It was both wonderful and hard to be so sensitive. And Benny was a man to try both ends of that. "We'll keep that in mind. You deserve to have your feelings respected."

Sawyer snuggled in.

"You didn't eat very much of your sandwich."

"Would you like it? You're welcome to it."

"No, I've had mine. I thought you were hungry too, though. And you look like you could handle a few more sandwiches."

"I probably could. This was hard, you know? Leaving everything and walking away. I was so scared."

"I bet. You should be very proud of taking this step. And look how it's turned out so far—you've found three amazing guys."

"I have, and now I have furniture." Sawyer ate a bite of sandwich.

"You do. It's a nice place. And you bought a king-size bed." He wiggled his eyebrows.

"I did. We fit if we snuggle."

"That's the joy of sleeping together, isn't it? The snuggling." Although to be honest, they often fucked and then fell right asleep.

"Yes. It's hard to learn to sleep alone."

"Yeah." He hugged Sawyer tight. "You don't have to sleep alone anymore. Unless you want to, of course."

"That's very kind. Seriously." Sawyer held him, resting them together.

"Have you had enough to eat?" He was ready to get back in bed, the snack having done the trick to tide him over.

"I have. I'll clean up, if you'd like to head back to bed."

"No, go ahead. I'll wait for you." He'd have suggested that Sawyer just leave it until morning but figured it would make the man twitchy if he didn't clean up first.

"Are you sure?" Sawyer cleaned up quickly, filling a large glass of water to take back with him.

Luke let the fact that he waited on Sawyer be his answer.

Sawyer smiled at him, his expression pleased.

When Sawyer was done, he put an arm around his shoulders and walked him back to bed. Derek had rolled into Sawyer's place, snuggled up against Benny. Which left him and Sawyer the right amount of space. He eased Sawyer into bed, then snuggled in close. Sawyer fit in all the right places. Luke set a kiss on Sawyer's shoulder. "You want a little help falling asleep?" He draped his hand over Sawyer's hip.

"Yes, Sir. Please." Sawyer moved closer to him.

He found Sawyer's mouth in the dark and licked at Sawyer's lips, then pressed his tongue in between them. The kiss was sweet, yielding, and he pushed in deeper. Sawyer tasted like honey, and Luke fucked the lovely lips, delving in deep. Sawyer let him in, moaning.

Luke crowded closer, undulating slowly to rub them together. He was learning the shape and sensation of Sawyer.

Derek groaned and turned over, nuzzled into Sawyer's neck. The boy really did have it bad.

Luke rolled his hips with stronger movements, pushing Sawyer into Derek so he was included.

"Mmm." Derek sighed, then began to snore again.

Luke laughed softly. "At least he didn't fart."

Sawyer's laugh answered his. "That might have knocked Benny to the floor."

"And that would have been bad." He hugged Sawyer to him, then took another kiss, opening Sawyer's lips with his tongue.

Images of the games they could play flittered through his mind, driving him to push a little deeper. He drove their bodies together with more force, loving the way their erections slid and bumped.

What a lovely, needy boy who had dropped into his lap.

He wrapped his hand around Sawyer's cock and began stroking, working it slowly. He was going to give Sawyer an orgasm to help him fall back to sleep. Sawyer's cock was long and lean, curving over his belly.

Groaning, he rubbed the tip, wanting to know if Sawyer liked a little sting across his slit or not.

Sawyer whimpered, bucking into his touch. Oh hell yes. He knew he could have a lot of fun with Sawyer. They all could. He rubbed across the tip of Sawyer's cock again, pressed his thumb against the slit, putting a bit of pressure on it.

Sawyer rolled into the touch, sweet boy begging for it.

"You ever played with sounds?" He tugged lightly on the head of Sawyer's cock. This needed a ring.

"Yes, Sir. I love cock play."

"Have you got your own?" Had Sawyer brought any of his toys with him? Or had he buried them with his master, figuratively speaking of course.

"No, Sir. I left everything. Everything."

"That means we can pick stuff out together." He could make Sawyer squirm, just from talking about it, from shopping. How fun.

He stroked Sawyer quickly, squeezing tight when he stroked near the head. Meanwhile, he reached for Sawyer's balls, rolling them.

"Sir." Sawyer curled, lips parted, so hungry.

He did appreciate the sound of that word. As much when Sawyer said it as when Benny said it, it seemed.

He slid his fingers behind Sawyer's balls and moaned when he found the guiche. Fuck yes.

"Oh, you are a treasure, aren't you?"

He could feel the heat of Sawyer's blush in response to his words, and that just made Sawyer even better. Humming happily, he tugged at the little ring as he slid his fingers across the tip of Sawyer's cock again. Yeah, they'd have a thick, heavy ring put right here so they could play.

"If it wasn't the middle of the night and we weren't doing this to help you get back to sleep, I would totally play. Keep you from coming even while I tease you unbearably."

Sawyer gasped, face going slack. "Please."

"Tomorrow. Right now you need to come and to sleep. But I promise you that you'll have your moments in the sun."

Heat poured over his fingers, slick and wet, Sawyer's eyes wide and bright.

"Mmm. There you go." He slowed the movements of his hand, watching Sawyer's face.

"Thank you." Sawyer melted, the expression pure bliss.

"Good night, baby boy." He kissed the corner of Sawyer's mouth. "Good night."

"I can't believe this is real." Sawyer's eyes closed, one tear escaping.

"Shh. Shh. Sleep. It'll still be real in the morning."

"Yes, Sir."

Poor broken boy. He wiped the tear away, kissing Sawyer's forehead.

He'd have to see what they could do to bring Sawyer back to himself again.

CHAPTER SIX

DEREK WOKE up squished and hot between Benny and Sawyer. He stayed where he was for a few minutes before the heat, the squish, and his bladder conspired to get him out of bed. He managed to climb over Benny without waking the big lug. Go him.

He padded naked to the bathroom, took care of his business, and drank some water. When he got back to bed, Benny had sprawled out, and there wasn't any space for him. That was okay; he was kind of awake at this point and would just toss and turn and wake everyone else.

So he headed for the kitchen. He was sure Sawyer wouldn't mind if he checked out the fridge and made himself something to eat.

Mmm… eggs, bacon, bread. All the important parts of breakfast.

He found a frying pan and put the whole package of bacon into it. Sawyer was going to have to buy some more—they were all big eaters. He put two slices of bread in the toaster to get that started, then cracked the eggs into a bowl to whisk with a bit of milk and some cheese.

Soft hands pressed against his waist. "Hey. Good morning."

Sawyer cuddled close.

He stopped what he was doing and smiled, reached back with his hand to touch Sawyer. "Good morning. I hope you don't mind I dove into your fridge."

"I don't mind. Seriously. Do you need help?"

"Sure. When that toast pops it needs buttering, and more toast put in."

Before Sawyer could go do that, though, Derek turned around and gave Sawyer a proper hug and an improper kiss. He was smiling when their lips finally parted.

"Now it's a good morning."

"Yes. Yes, it is." Sawyer hummed for him and reached up, stroked his lips.

"You're going to make me forget all about breakfast." That wasn't a bad thing, though.

"We don't want to waste the bacon, do we?"

"Well, you'd be worth burnt bacon."

"Oh, that's the sweetest thing I've ever heard."

That had him blushing a little. "Well, it's true."

Sawyer kissed him again, sweet and long, then turned to rescue the bacon. That gave him a great view of Sawyer's ass, and he grabbed it, fingers sliding over the lovely globes. Fuck, that was sweet.

"I could bend you over the table and make love to you."

Sawyer shivered for him, and he smiled.

"You like the sound of that? We haven't christened the table yet, after all."

"We haven't. Did you want toast still?"

"I want toast after. Too many crumbs if we're going to do this." Let it not be said he wasn't a considerate lover.

Sawyer began to chuckle. "I love your sense of humor."

He grinned at Sawyer. He hadn't actually been joking, but if he'd made Sawyer laugh, he was going to go with it.

"Do you want me on my back or my belly?"

"If you bend over the table, it's a great angle and I can hold on to your hips and pull you back into it, but if you're on your back, I can see your face."

"Decisions, decisions. What's your pleasure?"

"Your face. I want to be able to see your eyes, to kiss you." Maybe it was cheesy, but it was how he felt.

"I'd love that." Sawyer slipped his robe off, leaving himself bare.

"Look at you." He started touching, sliding his fingers over Sawyer's skin. He loved all the bare skin, the hints of marks from yesterday's games.

Sawyer looked up at him, and he pressed their lips together. God, every time he kissed this man it was like doing it for the first time all over again. He grabbed Sawyer's ass, squeezing him and lifting him to the table.

"Do I have to sneak back into the bedroom for supplies?"

"I don't have anything on me. I'm sorry."

"It's okay—you weren't exactly wearing anything with pockets." He giggled suddenly. "Or expecting to get jumped for breakfast."

"True. We should put a basket of supplies in here, hmm?"

"Maybe we should put a basket of supplies in every room." He grinned, feeling wicked, then kissed Sawyer. "Okay, gonna creep in and grab the stuff without waking the guys."

"Good luck with that." Sawyer's laughter followed him into the bedroom.

He smiled all the way to the headboard, where he found the stuff they needed. It was only as he turned to go back out that he noticed Luke and Benny watching him.

"Shoo," Luke told him. "We're busy here."

He was giggling as he went back out to the kitchen.

"What's funny?" Sawyer asked.

"We're not the only ones getting it on. I was sent summarily on my way after grabbing supplies."

Sawyer grinned and opened his arms. "Good for them."

"Uh-huh. We get to christen the kitchen table." He stepped in between Sawyer's legs and put the stuff down before wrapping his arms around Sawyer.

Sawyer held on to him, face lifted for a kiss. He gave it eagerly, gently rocking against Sawyer as they necked.

This was the best way ever to spend a morning—slow, lazy kisses, Sawyer open and naked. Derek approved.

He slid his hands along Sawyer's back, all the way down to his ass, which he grabbed and squeezed. He loved the way Sawyer felt in his hands. Loved it.

He finally stopped kissing long enough to drag his tongue along Sawyer's neck and down to his pierced nipples. The little rings were fascinating, and he tongued the right one first, then the left.

He tested them with his teeth, gently at first, then a bit harder. Sawyer jerked and cried out. He knew Sawyer liked it because he pushed toward Derek instead of pulling away from him.

That made him tug harder.

Sweet. He loved how Sawyer heated up for him. And the sounds Sawyer made went straight to his balls, spurring on his need.

God, he needed in. He needed to be wrapped in Sawyer's perfect ass.

He slowly eased Sawyer onto his back on the table. The height was just right for him. All he had to do was tug a little and Sawyer's ass was right at the edge of the table, little hole there for him.

"You okay?" He hoped it would be comfortable enough.

"I am. I want you."

The words settled in his balls, increasing his need. They made him happy too. That Sawyer wanted him felt amazing. He grabbed the lube from where he'd set it and opened the tube to get some slick stuff on his fingers. He rubbed them together, getting them slippery, then pressed one against Sawyer's hole. He played for a moment, pushing but not going in, before letting it sink in all the way.

"Mmm...." Sawyer's face relaxed. He loved how Sawyer enjoyed ass play.

He slid his finger in and out for a bit, then slicked all his fingers back up and pushed two in this time. In and curl up, then out, then in again and spread apart, then twist and turn. He kept varying things, pushing in more lube and opening Sawyer up but playing while he was doing it. He could watch Sawyer enjoying this all day long.

Sawyer was hard and dripping, and there was no question he could make Sawyer come like this. If he didn't want to be buried inside Sawyer so badly, he would have done it just to watch.

Good thing they had time to try again.

"You ready?" he asked as he pulled his fingers away and grabbed a condom.

"So ready. I ache for you."

"I do like the sound of that." He got the condom on and slicked it up. Then he pushed into the little hole he'd prepped. He watched Sawyer's face as he did, loving the open need, the way the dark flush climbed up Sawyer's belly.

He sank all the way in, then stayed there for a moment, leaned in and took a quick kiss.

Sawyer wrapped those lean legs around his waist, drawing him in closer. Groaning, he began to rock, doing the push-and-pull dance of making love. Sawyer slid on the table, the slick surface squeaking.

Chuckling, he grabbed hold of Sawyer's hips, pulling him into each thrust.

"P-polishing the table?" Sawyer was laughing with him.

"Uh-huh. Yeah." He slammed in, hoping to hit Sawyer's gland.

He tilted Sawyer's hips, and then he found it, Sawyer's shoulders leaving the table. He kept pumping, hitting the same spot over and over.

Sawyer began to cry out, the sound loud, unmuffled. Derek loved that, and it had him thrusting harder. He wanted Sawyer to make a lot of noise. He wanted to be the reason for each sound.

He wanted Luke and Benny to hear what he was doing to Sawyer.

Groaning, he dug his fingers into Sawyer's skin and tugged him back as hard as possible.

"Oh God!" Sawyer sat up, slamming down onto his cock.

"Yes! Come on my cock!"

Sawyer cried out, arching impossibly as spunk sprayed between them. The tightening of Sawyer's body around his cock sent him over the edge, and he matched Sawyer's cry as he filled the condom.

"Look at that. You look debauched. It's hot." Benny was wrapped around Luke, watching them from the doorway.

Derek was startled by Benny's voice, but not in a bad way, and he stayed where he was, buried inside Sawyer and holding on to him.

"We were making breakfast." He smiled at Sawyer as he said it.

"We were." Sawyer's ass squeezed him tight.

He groaned and kissed Sawyer again, lazy and wet and delicious.

He barely heard Luke and Benny's laughter through the wonderful haze of Sawyer's kiss.

Sawyer kissed him like there was nothing on earth he wanted to do more, the connection drugging, heady. One kiss turned into a second and then a third, his cock staying hard.

God, he could go for a twofer. He should probably change out the condom first, but then he'd have to come out, and right now he didn't want to do anything more than kiss Sawyer and roll his hips. Sawyer seemed to be on the same page, legs still wrapped around him, hands in his hair.

Speaking of hands, there were extras at his hips and fingers wrapped around the base of his cock as he was tugged away from Sawyer's hole. He whimpered against Sawyer's lips, trying to push back in.

"Easy, Derek. We're just helping you with your rubber situation." Luke licked his earlobe, body warm against his back.

He kept kissing Sawyer and let them take off the condom and put on a new one. Benny's hand was rough as he spread more lube on. Then they lined him back up with Sawyer's hole, and Luke gave his ass a pat.

With a groan, Derek pushed back into Sawyer. Oh fuck, that was perfect.

Sawyer groaned, ass rippling around him. "Yes."

"Uh-huh." He dove back in for more kisses, moving his hips in small increments. He was totally willing to draw this time out for longer. Benny nestled up behind him, warm and snuggly, fingers finding his nipples unerringly.

He groaned, and the sound was answered by Sawyer. God, this was so good. He rocked a little faster, finding a new rhythm.

Fuck, he could do this for hours, for days. Years.

Benny kept tugging at his nipples, then added playing with his balls to the mix. Okay, he probably wouldn't be able to last for hours, certainly not for days, not with Benny's added touches.

He was going to try, though. He was totally going to try.

He focused on Sawyer's mouth and Sawyer's ass, and he was lost in both, drowning in the sensations of making love to this man.

Sawyer gripped his prick, milking it over and over. It was so good it made him whimper, and he pushed in harder, wanting to get Sawyer's gland, to make his lover as crazy for it as he was. Again.

To make Sawyer wild again.

He broke the kiss, gasping for breath as Benny rocked behind him, rubbing his hard-on against Derek's lower back.

"Fuck. Fuck, this is…." He panted against Sawyer's lips.

"It is," Sawyer agreed. "More. More. More."

Yeah, he got that. And he gave it, moving faster, filling Sawyer over and over.

God, he was glad this table was new.

And sturdy.

And that Sawyer loved getting reamed.

He sucked on Sawyer's upper lip, bit at it. He opened and closed his fingers on Sawyer's skin.

"Need this," Sawyer whispered. "So much."

He loved that, loved that he was giving Sawyer what he needed.

"For you." He'd go as long as Sawyer needed him to.

"So sweet," Benny teased. "So sweet."

He reached back with one hand and swatted the side of Benny's ass. Luke's laughter battled with Benny's groan.

Then he turned his attention back to Sawyer and the way their bodies fit together so well. Sawyer was watching him, staring at him with burning eyes.

So intense. So deep. He stared right back.

Oh, Sawyer was… something else. And Derek wanted very badly to keep him.

"Derek. Kiss me. Please."

He'd gotten so lost in Sawyer's eyes, he'd forgotten to keep kissing him. Grinning, he pressed their mouths together.

Sawyer groaned into his mouth, ass gripping Derek's cock tight. He swallowed the sounds and fed them back to Sawyer.

Benny kept touching him, stroking his ass, encouraging his thrusts. It was maddening in the best way possible, and it kept him moving, spurred him on.

"Touch me…," Sawyer begged. "Please."

He reached for Sawyer's cock, finding Luke had beaten him to it.

Luke's chuckle was warm, and he took Derek's hand and wrapped it around Sawyer's flesh. Then he wrapped his hand around Derek's and moved them. Which worked because it meant Derek didn't have to think about it at all.

Luke had him working the tip of Sawyer's cock, rubbing it almost harshly. He'd have never done it that hard on his own, but Sawyer bucked and whimpered, ass like a vise around his cock. Fuck. So good.

"See how much he needs it, Derek?"

He did see. More than that, he *felt* how much Sawyer needed the touch. He rubbed the tip again, pressing his thumb against the lips of Sawyer's slit, kept playing with it, Luke keeping their hands moving up and down the hot column of flesh. Sawyer's muscles rippled around his cock.

Derek whimpered. "Oh God. So good."

"Soon. Soon, Derek, please."

"Yes. Please. Now." He was so ready, his body surging toward his orgasm. He squeezed the tip of Sawyer's cock, twisted hard, and Sawyer shot for him.

Sawyer's body demanded his orgasm in return, and he jerked in a few more times before freezing and filling the second condom.

God. God, so good.

His eyes rolled up in his head, and he panted. He and Sawyer rested their foreheads together as they slowly caught their breath.

Meanwhile, Luke and Benny helped them with getting rid of the condom, and he'd be damned if he didn't hear the toaster pop and the sound of food cooking. Nice.

"Fabulous breakfast, hmm?" Sawyer whispered.

"Best breakfast I've had in… ever," he whispered right back. He slid his hands along Sawyer's back.

"Yeah. Ever." Sawyer arched into him.

"You two can't be ready to go again already!" Benny slapped his ass. "I'm trying to set the table here. Too many naked butts for breakfast."

Derek snorted, the sound turning into laughter.

"Sweats for all, then?"

"I'm pretty sure any of yours are not going to even pretend to fit Luke." Derek thought it would be funny to watch him try them on, though.

"No. Not any of you, if I'm honest."

"Then we'll just have to risk our butts. And your chairs, I guess." He giggled, imagining them all naked on the new dining room chairs.

"I can always grab towels...." Sawyer's laugh filled the air as Benny grabbed him and tickled him.

"I'll get them," Derek suggested. He thought Sawyer would prefer the towels to their naked butts. They were brand-new chairs, after all.

"Snap to it, then, Derek. The food's seconds from being ready."

Derek saluted Luke, gave Sawyer and Benny a warm smile, and went to the linen closet in the hall next to Sawyer's bedroom. There were indeed towels in there, emerald green and ruby red, all looking fluffy and new. He grabbed four, putting one back when he realized it was one of those tiny hand towels and replacing it with another larger one. Then he went back to the kitchen with them.

"Oh, those are beautiful."

"They're new. I wanted something amazing."

"To match the one who owns them." Derek touched Sawyer's cheek.

Benny shook his head. "Good God, that was the cheesiest thing I've ever heard."

Derek stuck his tongue out at Benny.

"It was dear." Sawyer leaned into his touch. "Thank you."

Derek beamed. Sawyer made him feel good, plain and simple. Hell, even just being around him felt good. He leaned in for a kiss.

"Save it for later. Breakfast is served." Luke put four plates piled high with eggs, bacon, toast, and beans around the table. God knew where the last had come from, but they were a perfect fit for Luke's "full breakfast." Especially when he put a plate of toasted waffles in the middle of the table as well.

"Oh, beautiful!" Sawyer applauded, and both Luke and Benny blushed.

It looked like he wasn't the only one who thought Sawyer was sweet and wonderful.

He pulled out one of the chairs for Sawyer, making sure one of the towels went down first.

Benny sat. "Thanks, Dee."

He rolled his eyes and pulled out a second chair.

Luke sat. "Thanks, Dee."

What the hell? This time he shook his head, but he pulled out the third chair. At least he knew Sawyer would get to sit in this one.

Benny and Luke were chuckling at him.

"Do you want this one, Derek?"

"Sit, Sawyer."

Sawyer sat.

He let his fingers slide across Sawyer's shoulders, then sat in the last chair. The food looked good, but he had to admit to being distracted by Sawyer. He just couldn't turn his gaze away.

"NRE," Luke said.

"What?"

"New relationship energy. It's like a drug."

He reached for Sawyer's hand and twined their fingers together. "I don't care what you call it." He didn't even care that it was hard to eat like this.

Sawyer held on, hand warm in his.

"Eat," Luke ordered. "I didn't cook so it could get cold and then thrown out."

"Technically, I made the bacon and mixed together the eggs," Derek pointed out.

"I will put your lover over my knee if you argue." Luke fixed Derek with a look. Then, "Eat," Luke said again, putting a little something in the words that had him grabbing his fork and scooping up a forkful of eggs.

Benny groaned. "Love it when you get all toppy."

Sawyer bent to his food, noshing quietly.

Derek squeezed his hand, hoping Luke and Benny's banter wasn't bothering him. Sawyer looked up, grinned at him. "Hey."

He smiled right back. "How's the bacon?"

"Perfect. I love it crunchy."

He didn't even care if Sawyer was lying to make him feel good. He leaned in and took a salty, bacon-tinged kiss. "Thank you."

"I like mine crunchy too," Benny noted.

Derek laughed and blew him a kiss. "Thank you too."

Benny grinned at him, eyes twinkling.

"You are such a tease," Derek accused fondly. He usually was too, but something about Sawyer made him protective.

"I am." Benny stuck his tongue out, waggling it at him.

"I'm gonna come get that," Derek told Benny. He didn't, though. He just kept holding on to Sawyer's hand.

"I can do it." Sawyer leaned over and kissed the corner of Benny's mouth.

Oh. He was one part jealous, but more parts turned on.

Then Sawyer came to him, kissed the corner of his mouth. He turned his face, chasing Sawyer's lips, wanting a proper kiss. Sawyer gave it to him, moaning into his lips. He opened up, letting Sawyer in. Oh, mapley goodness. He loved it.

"Don't you think you should both finish your breakfast before you go for round... three? Four?" Luke asked.

"It's at least three," Benny agreed.

"Come sit in my lap and we'll eat, Sawyer." Derek was almost still talking when Sawyer landed in his lap.

He grinned, his lips still curled in a smile when Sawyer kissed him.

"Lord, Luke. They're insatiable."

"I know. It's sexy as hell, isn't it?"

"I guess so, yeah."

"You guess so?" Luke laughed. "I know you're a better voyeur than that."

"Can I sit with you, then?"

"Baby, you don't have to ask me twice. Especially as you've finished your plate. Come sit and help me decide what to get these sexy guys to do for us." The chair scraped along the floor as Luke sat back from the table.

Benny pushed into Luke's arms with a happy moan. Derek smiled and popped a piece of bacon into Sawyer's mouth. He liked watching too, and Benny and Luke were so hot together.

"Mmm." Sawyer crunched down happily.

He leaned in to lick a bacon crumb off Sawyer's lips.

"Derek...." There was a clear warning in Luke's tone.

He gave Luke a cheeky glance, grabbing another piece of bacon and munching on it himself. He had this. They would eat and feel each other up at the same time. He could totally multitask. Sawyer leaned into him, tongue sliding over his skin, teasing his throat.

He groaned. Okay, he could multitask, but damn, Sawyer was drawing his entire focus. His breath huffed out of him. "You want a toaster waffle, Sa-Sawyer?"

"Hmm?" Sawyer kept kissing.

He grabbed one blindly and took a bite. "Toaster waffle." His words were muffled by the waffle; he was trying to pay enough attention to eat it.

Sawyer moaned against his throat.

He kept hold of the waffle, even as he dropped his head back, giving Sawyer more room to continue making magic against his throat. He'd tried, and that counted, right?

"You're begging for trouble, Derek." Luke chuckled.

"Hey, I tried." He couldn't do better than that. Sawyer was close and cuddling with him, biting and licking at his throat. "Are you hungry, Sawyer?" he asked, making one last effort to prove he was following Luke's directive.

"Mm-hmm." Sawyer bit his earlobe.

He gasped softly at the sensation, his hand tightening on Sawyer. "Not for food," he guessed. He didn't mind at all being what Sawyer wanted to eat.

"I just... now that I know I can."

"Huh?" He wasn't sure if he was too engrossed in what Sawyer was doing or if Sawyer wasn't being coherent, but he didn't know what Sawyer meant. As long as Sawyer kept licking and kissing him, he didn't think he cared.

"I know I can touch, taste. Now."

"You can have me to do that anytime you want." He slid his hand along Sawyer's back.

Sawyer pushed in closer, the constant hum driving him mad.

He moaned, humping up a little to get some contact on his prick.

"Why don't we take this to the bedroom?" Luke suggested.

"Mmm." Benny stole another bite of bacon. "Sounds perfect."

Sawyer made a noise that probably meant yes, but he didn't stop what he was doing, and Derek swallowed hard, totally undone by the sucking kisses, his body feeling like it was electrified.

Luke grinned at him, shook his head. "We're going to have to give you Dom training, Derek."

"Huh?" He blinked over at Luke. What?

"You heard me." Luke winked at him.

"I wasn't really paying attention," he admitted. And who could blame him? Luke was way over there while Sawyer was in his lap, making him crazy.

"We'll chat later. Bed?"

"Uh-huh." That he got. He wrapped his hands around Sawyer's ass and stood.

"So strong," Sawyer whispered against his lips.

He smiled and would have preened, but that was hard to do with his arms full of man. Besides, falling would so suck.

Luke and Benny moved ahead of him, hands on each other's asses as they walked. He had his hands on Sawyer's ass too.

It was like an assapalooza.

He snorted and laughed at himself.

"What's funny?" Sawyer didn't sound like he really cared.

"Just having an assapalooza moment."

"Assapawhat?"

"Assapalooza—you know, like a festival of asses?" He was trying hard to say it with a straight face, but Luke and Benny were killing themselves laughing at him.

Sawyer's laugh was soft, tickling his throat.

They got to the bed, and he stood there with Sawyer wrapped around him. He couldn't figure out an easy way to lie down on the bed without letting go of Sawyer, so he simply stood there, holding on happily.

Luke turned him around and helped him sit, Sawyer ending up on his lap.

"Oh, there we are."

Luke patted his back. "You are love-stupid, aren't you?"

"Hey, that's not nice." Derek stuck his tongue out at Luke.

"It wasn't nasty. You're addled, and I'm guessing it's from the bundle in your arms." Luke grinned at him. "There's nothing wrong with that."

"I do feel like I've been bowled over." He looked at Sawyer, smiling into his eyes. "I'm not complaining, I like it. You... you make me feel things. Make me want things." Derek laughed. "You make me forget things."

"We'll make lists. Don't worry."

"Oh man, I wasn't organized before. Are you going to organize me?" He laughed again and squeezed Sawyer. "I like the way we fit." He meant physically and not-physically too. He liked how Sawyer's mind worked, how gentle and calm he was.

"You could go back to what you were doing now," he told Sawyer. Now that they were safely set.

"Mmm. I can." Sawyer nuzzled in, loving on him with gentle lips.

"I think I could die happy if this was going on."

"I want to be fucking when I go," Benny declared.

Luke laughed and grabbed Benny, kissing him hard. "That's my boy."

It occurred to him talking about dying might not be sitting well with Sawyer. "You okay?" he whispered.

"Yeah. Yeah, I'm okay." Sawyer kissed his cheek.

"Cool." He turned his face, catching Sawyer's lips with his own. As they were kissing, he lay back onto the mattress.

Sawyer ended up draped over him, legs straddling him. It let him drag his hands along Sawyer's spine and grab his most-grabbable ass. He squeezed, loving the way the flesh gave beneath his fingertips.

He tapped the well-fucked hole, loving how it was hot and swollen under his touch.

"You wanna sixty-nine?" He'd love to sink into that again, but he didn't want to hurt Sawyer.

"Whatever you want, Derek."

"You could plug him," Luke murmured.

Sawyer bucked against him at Luke's words. "I haven't got any plugs, Luke." He knew Luke did, but they were upstairs.

"Mmm. Let's go pick one out for Sawyer, Benny."

"You like that kinky stuff a lot, huh?" And how did Luke always know? He was a sex ninja or something. Dom—that was the word.

"I do. So does Sawyer."

Did that mean Sawyer was going to like Luke better than him? He didn't like that thought at all.

"Shh…." Sawyer stroked his forehead. "I don't need anything. It's okay."

"I can be kinky. I'm just not… amazing like Luke."

"Sawyer's right. It's okay." Luke ran his fingers through Derek's hair. "We're all going to find how we fit and make things work."

"Right now, we'll just be like this, huh?" Sawyer kissed him, the touch gentle, soft. Then Sawyer began to slide down, disappearing under the covers to lap at his cock.

"Oh God."

Luke chuckled and kissed him gently. Then Luke and Benny headed out, leaving him with Sawyer.

"Sixty-nine?" he said softly. He wanted Sawyer to get pleasure out of this too.

"Mmm… please." Sawyer kept nuzzling his prick.

"Gonna need you to come up here, then. Well, the lower parts." He groaned as Sawyer hit a sensitive spot. "Oh damn. Fuck."

Sawyer chuckled and focused on that hot spot. Moaning at the pleasure, he made grabby hands for Sawyer to come up so he could reciprocate. Stubborn, teasing, wonderful man.

Sawyer slowly turned, mouth sliding all the way down his cock. Gasping, he bucked, his body moving entirely without his permission. His cock went deep into Sawyer's throat, and he pulled back.

"Sorry, sorry. I couldn't help it."

"Mmm… I won't break."

"No? That's good." He didn't want to break Sawyer. He just wanted to use him hard and put him away wet. Groaning, he wrapped his hands around Sawyer's thighs and helped him turn the last little bit. That put Sawyer's needy cock right at his mouth, and he leaned slightly forward, licking across the tip. Then he went back, tongue lingering on Sawyer's slit, tasting the precome there. Sawyer was pulling at him fiercely, sucking enough that he had to force himself to focus.

His balls ached, and it felt so good. He found himself pushing, hips dancing as he tried to get more. Sawyer kept giving him more and more, never letting up.

He got the tip of Sawyer's cock between his lips and began to suck, hoping to give as good as he was getting. If he had to, he'd pay Sawyer back, right? Right.

Derek slapped Sawyer's cockhead with his tongue, looking to stimulate Sawyer's slit. Oh. Oh, he felt Sawyer's cry. So he stayed right there, teasing the little slit with his tongue. He worked it as best he could and still suck a little at the same time. Salt fell on his tongue, tantalizing him and encouraging him to work harder. He pulled and dragged his tongue over the slit, wanting to make Sawyer need. It was like a race where they would both be winners.

Sawyer pointed his tongue and pressed it into his slit, and Derek cried out around Sawyer's cock as he shot.

Sawyer took him, never backing away. He panted, trying to catch his breath, which made it hard to suck, but he managed to keep his mouth wrapped around Sawyer's cock even as he shuddered through a couple of delicious aftershocks.

Sawyer tasted like heaven—male and hot and warm. And he was soon focused on that, on bringing Sawyer pleasure. Sawyer whimpered, cheek on his thigh, hips moving restlessly.

He sucked harder, resolved to give Sawyer what he needed. Sawyer dropped little kisses against him, sharp bites that made him jump. So many different sensations, and Sawyer seemed determined to offer them all to him. It almost seemed like Sawyer's pleasure was secondary.

"It's your turn, Sawyer," he muttered. He wasn't selfish; he wanted to make Sawyer wild for him.

He slid his fingers between Sawyer's thighs and fondled Sawyer's balls. Sawyer spread, bucking up into his touch.

Bingo! He rolled Sawyer's balls now, his touch a little on the rough side.

"D-Derek!" Sawyer shifted, hips pressing the sweet cock into his mouth.

He was assuming that meant it had been a good touch, so he sucked harder than ever and did it again, nudging the sensitive orbs fairly hard.

Sawyer shuddered, crying out and grabbing at his legs.

Derek loved that he'd found something that could make Sawyer as crazy as he'd been not two minutes ago.

He moaned deep in his chest as Sawyer fucked his mouth. He swallowed whenever he could, knowing he'd loved that so much when Sawyer had done it to him. He was learning a lot about giving pleasure to Sawyer in a very short period of time. Sawyer was... special.

That thought put an extra oomph in his sucking, and he gave Sawyer even more.

"Soon. Soon, please. Soon."

He tapped on Sawyer's hole, pressing hard for a moment.

Seed filled his mouth, hot and wet and salty. He swallowed as best as he could, trying not to gag.

He didn't want Sawyer to think he was grossed out. Because he wasn't. He grabbed hold of Sawyer's ass, squeezing it happily.

"God. So good." The moan suited him all the way to the bone.

He pressed a kiss to the tip of Sawyer's cock, then rubbed it along his cheek.

Sawyer hummed, cuddling into him with a happy little sigh. Grabbing Sawyer's arm, he tugged him back up into place. He wanted a kiss, wanted to taste himself in Sawyer's mouth and share Sawyer's taste with him.

"Mmm... hello, Derek." Sawyer dove right into his kiss.

God, this man blew his mind. Wrapping his arms around Sawyer, he kissed Sawyer right back. This was... special. Sawyer was special.

"You two do make the room sizzle," Luke said.

Obviously the guys were back.

"We got a pretty plug for you to shove up your boyfriend's ass." Benny was the epitome of romance.

Luke swatted Benny's ass, the sound loud, and Derek leaned his and Sawyer's foreheads together as he started to laugh.

Sawyer curled in, staying mostly hidden under the blankets.

"Do you want the plug?" Derek asked, focusing on Sawyer. This was about Sawyer, not about Luke.

"I don't want to make you uncomfortable."

"I'm good with it, as long as it's what you want. I don't want to make you do anything you don't want to." Look at them, a kinky Henry James gift they had going here.

"I know how to say no." That was sure.

"Cool, then let's do this." He held his hand out for the plug, eyes going wide when Luke gave it to him. "It's big!" Like really big. Surprisingly big.

"He can take it, Dee. Think about how he'll walk with it in."

The sudden visual was stunning, and he moaned. Benny always had an extra sexy wiggle in his walk when he was plugged. Sawyer was extra sexy to start with, so whoa. And also wow. And also, okay, he was suddenly way on board. Given Sawyer was a happy participant.

"I need a lot of lube." He moaned as he held the toy. "Tell me that you want this, man?"

"I-I want it."

"Then you'll have it." He kissed Sawyer and rolled them, putting Sawyer beneath him. "Gotta open you first." He held his hand out in the international signal of "lube me up."

"Are you going to let us watch?" Benny asked.

"That's up to Sawyer."

"You're hot together. I want to watch. What do you say, Sawyer? You into being on display?"

Sawyer's cheeks went bright red, and he didn't say yes, but he didn't say no either.

Wow. And he'd been worried Sawyer would find their arrangement… unseemly.

He gave Sawyer a grin. "Let's give them a show, babe."

He eased the blankets away, exposing the lean body. God, Sawyer was gorgeous. He slid his hand along the long lines. "So pretty."

Sawyer pinked and arched toward his touch. "Thank you."

He kissed Sawyer quickly, then held his hand out again. "Is someone gonna give me the lube, already?" If they were going to have an audience, the least Luke and Benny could do was help him out.

"God, pushy." Benny pressed close and squirted lube on his fingers.

"I know what I need, that's all."

Luke chuckled. "There's a Dom there inside you, Derek."

"I don't even know what that means, man."

"You will." Luke patted his shoulder.

Derek rolled his eyes, but he had a smile for Sawyer. "Gonna open you up, get you good and slick."

"How do you want me?"

"Like this. I want to see your face."

Sawyer nodded, gaze never leaving his face.

He kept staring at Sawyer as he reached down and slid his fingers along Sawyer's flesh, headed for that sweet hole. Sawyer stretched out, one leg spreading wide. Letting him in. No. Inviting him in. How hot was that? Pretty fucking.

Groaning, he sank a single finger into Sawyer's body, the tight heat wrapping around him immediately.

Sweet, swollen—the wrinkled hole sucked him in. He began fingerfucking Sawyer, sinking deep each time until he pushed another finger in with the first. They'd fucked already, so Sawyer didn't need him to be gentle.

He quickly added a third finger, pushing more lube into Sawyer at the same time.

"Benny? Hold his legs open?" Luke murmured.

Derek was still watching Sawyer's face, so he knew the idea wasn't repugnant to Sawyer. He kept going.

It was easier to touch with Sawyer held wide, he had to admit. Easier to watch too.

He pushed his fingers deep, looking for Sawyer's gland. As soon as he found it, Sawyer gasped, stomach flushing dark.

"Right there, huh?" He touched that spot a few more times, loving the expression on Sawyer's face.

"Uh... uh-huh. There."

"Got it. Got you." He grinned, gazing happily into Sawyer's eyes.

"Don't forget what you're in there for," Luke murmured.

"What? Oh! Yeah. I guess you're slick enough for the plug."

Sawyer clenched, gripping his fingers and keeping him deep.

"Okay, baby, I can stay in a while longer." He liked that Sawyer wanted him over the plug.

Sawyer smiled at him, eyes unfocused, gaze soft.

He dropped another gentle kiss on Sawyer's lips, lingering for a moment. He loved how Sawyer tasted; it was a part of what made his kisses magical, along with how Sawyer opened right up to him.

Derek lost himself in the kiss, fingers moving inside Sawyer as he drowned in Sawyer's taste. God, he could do this forever. Sawyer worked with him, taking him deep time and again, ass muscles rippling and tugging at his fingers.

He wriggled his fingers, pushing back against Sawyer's grip in an effort to bring as much pleasure as possible. He tugged his fingers halfway out and pushed back to hit Sawyer's gland over and over as their kisses deepened, got harder and hotter.

"Jesus, they're on fire," Benny whispered.

That was for sure what it felt like, and he hoped they blazed forever.

"Uh-huh. Put some more lube in, Derek. So he doesn't dry out."

"Mmm." He heard, but those kisses....

Suddenly, Luke tugged his hand away and coated his fingers with more lube. Then Luke set his fingers back against Sawyer's hole. Sawyer bucked, taking them back in. The way was super slick again, and Sawyer clamped down around him. The way Sawyer jerked and rocked made his eyes roll back in his head.

It wasn't long before Luke tugged his fingers out again, this time putting the already lubed-up plug into his hand. Damn, he'd been fine with his fingers, but he supposed they couldn't actually do this forever. The plug was heavy, fat, something Sawyer couldn't ignore.

It seemed Sawyer didn't want to either, body moving, bearing down to take the plug in. Derek actually backed out of the kiss to watch. Sawyer really was stunning, and like this he was utterly magical.

The tiny hole began to spread, to stretch around the plug. He pushed a little, giving Sawyer something to push against. Sawyer bucked and took more in, and Derek moaned, pushing a little harder so suddenly a quarter of the plug had disappeared into Sawyer's body.

He gasped softly as he watched Sawyer take it, begin to swallow the plug.

"Fuck, you're amazing," Derek murmured, eyes flashing back to Sawyer's face and seeing nothing but pleasure and need.

"He is," Luke agreed, one hand sliding along Derek's back, the other over Sawyer's bent leg. "He has a hungry little hole, doesn't he?"

"He does. You do." He smiled at Sawyer—grinned, really. He was excited and turned on and falling in love.

Oh. Oh wow. Falling in love.

How fucking cool.

Groaning, he pushed the plug in deeper, rocking their bodies together as he did.

Luke's lips brushed his ear. "When you get it to the widest part, stop."

His gaze shot over to Luke, who smiled and nodded and mouthed, "Trust me."

So when he'd worked the plug in to the widest point—and wow, there was already a lot of it inside Sawyer—he stopped moving it.

Sawyer moaned, and Derek leaned back, staring. Look at that. Sawyer's ring was spread wide, stretched beautifully.

He whimpered softly and touched Sawyer's skin, sliding his finger along the stretched flesh. Burning and silky and utterly amazing.

Sawyer arched, and Benny pulled Sawyer's knees up higher. Derek bent and licked all around the stretched skin.

"Fuck! Fuck, please!"

Oh… that gave him a rush of need.

Moaning, he kept licking as Sawyer jumped against the sheets. God, Derek wanted more of those noises. Making Sawyer need was one of his new favorite things.

"Twist the plug, Derek."

He did. And Sawyer went wild. So he did it again, with more force this time.

"Can I kiss him?" Benny asked.

Derek looked at Sawyer—that was totally his decision, not Derek's.

Sawyer moaned and reached for Benny.

Bending, Benny pressed their lips together. Sawyer opened, and Benny went to town, devouring Sawyer's mouth. Derek had to admit, from down between Sawyer's legs, looking up, that was fucking hot.

"We're going to have so much fun, Dee. I swear to God," Luke said.

He rose up and kissed Luke, taking the words right out of his mouth. Then he went back to alternately twisting the plug and licking at Sawyer's stretched skin.

Sawyer was wild against him, crying out into Benny's mouth. Luke's fingers slid along Derek's spine, and suddenly all four of them were connected, touching and bringing each other pleasure.

Derek's entire body felt like it was on fire, lit up. He left Sawyer's ass in favor of licking his way up along Sawyer's cock, using his tongue to fiddle with the little slit at the tip. As he was doing that, he pushed the plug the rest of the way in.

Seed sprayed from Sawyer, his lover going wild underneath him. He caught some of it on his face and licked what he could reach off, groaning at the flavor that filled his mouth. Sawyer sobbed, clinging to Benny, to him. He thought it was a good thing, but he looked to Luke to make sure Luke thought so too.

Luke nodded, then put Derek's hands on Sawyer, encouraging him to pet. He loved touching Sawyer, so that wasn't a hardship at all. He stroked the slender but surprisingly cut belly and slid his fingers across the hard little nipples with their rings.

He tugged a little hard, twisting. Sawyer gasped and grabbed his arms, holding on to him like he was the only solid thing in the universe. He tugged again, then moved to the other nipple, going a little softer with this one.

"Mmm. Derek…."

"Yeah, baby. I'm right here." He leaned in and gave each little nip a kiss. Then he pressed their lips together, Benny's closeness adding heat to the mix. Benny licked his earlobe, lapping gently. He shivered, driving his body against Sawyer. God, it was intense and electric and impossible. Needing to come again so badly, so soon after having just come. Like twice.

Sawyer reached down, grabbed at his cock, and stroked him firmly. He nodded. Yeah. Yeah, he wanted that so fucking badly. Benny's hand joined Sawyer's, helping out, gripping harder.

He whimpered, dropping his head and panting as they worked him.

Luke whispered in his ear. "Fuck, this is magic."

He managed to nod. He couldn't agree more.

Luke wrapped around him from behind, body hot, cock hotter where it rubbed against his lower back. He rocked back and forth, riding both hands and that strong body. It felt so fucking good, and he wanted more. He rocked faster, taking what he needed.

Sawyer squeezed hard, thumb dragging over his slit.

"Fuck!" That was all he needed. He came, his balls emptying quick and hard.

Sawyer rubbed the seed in, slicking his shaft. He hissed, his skin sensitive and Sawyer's touch so huge. Immediately, that touch eased, Sawyer paying attention to him.

He found Sawyer's mouth, kissing his thanks before collapsing onto the bed, part of his weight on this amazing man.

"Wow." Benny grinned at him, looking mischievous as hell.

"Uh-huh." He didn't have words, but he couldn't disagree. He put a kiss on Sawyer's cheek.

"Damn, you two were on fire." Luke's chuckle was husky, teasing.

He rubbed cheeks with Sawyer. "Yeah. Yeah, burning up. You good, babe?"

"Mmm. Full."

Yeah, he imagined so. That was a hell of a plug. Sawyer sounded pretty damn blissed-out, though.

"You two want a nap, I bet," Luke noted.

Derek smiled against Sawyer's skin. "A snuggle at least. Sawyer's a champion snuggler." He loved that about Sawyer.

"I want you, Luke." Benny eased over Sawyer, shoving him a little bit.

Derek wriggled himself and Sawyer to the side of the bed to give Luke and Benny more room to get their groove on. "You wanna watch?" he asked Sawyer. "They're super hot together."

"Long as I can stay right here."

"That's the plan." He wrapped his arms tightly around Sawyer, and Sawyer snuggled in, plugged butt pressing into the curve of his hips.

It was hot and cozy and just about perfect. Eyes half-closed, he watched Luke love on Benny.

CHAPTER SEVEN

SAWYER CLEANED the kitchen and got to work once the guys left. He made himself stop thinking and wondering and worrying, and he just wrote.

> A set of four coffee mugs in a ~~horrible~~ lovely shade of ~~bilious neon green~~ peridot with delicate handles that are guaranteed to ~~snap right off~~ make your morning cup of coffee ~~taste less like ass~~ a joy.

Man, he wasn't in the mood for this.

He sighed and went back to worrying about whether he'd just utterly fucked up by getting involved with all of his neighbors.

There was a knock on the door, a sharp rat-a-tat. "Sawyer? It's me," Derek called out.

"Come on in." He was going to stay at his desk and at least pretend to be working.

Derek entered, looking sexy, hot, and easy in his skin. He gave Sawyer a brilliant smile. "Hey, babe."

"Hey, you. How's your day going?" *I'm restless, plugged, and stressed-out.*

"I missed you. I know it's only been a day, but you were all I could think of at work. I didn't get anything done." Derek didn't look particularly upset about that as he came over.

"You didn't taste anything good?"

"Nothing as good as you." Derek bent and licked his cheek before closing their mouths together in a kiss.

Derek tasted like heaven, male and right and rich. Their tongues played together, and he was as loath to end the kiss as Derek seemed to be.

He wasn't sure what the dynamic was among all of them, but he knew that Derek fascinated him.

Derek finally parted their lips and rested their foreheads together. "Mmm. Definitely the best thing I've tasted all day. So what have you been up to?"

"Trying to work. I just find myself sort of bleh about it."

"Hard to write soppy greeting cards if you're feeling bleh, huh?" Derek kissed his nose. "I have an idea or two on how to make you feel less bleh."

"Catalog copy today, but yeah. And also, yeah?"

Derek waggled his eyebrow. "Oh yeah." The word was drawn out, sexy. Then Derek grinned and wagged his eyebrows in an entirely different way. "You wanna play No Oxygen Included?"

"No Oxygen what?" He grinned. He'd do whatever. Maybe it would clear his head.

"It's a new game. It's called No Oxygen Included. Come on over and I'll show you. And then we'll make each other feel amazing."

"Okay. Sure. I like to play games."

"I know." Derek took his hand and twined their fingers together, leading him across the hall to his own apartment. "I like playing with you."

"I like you." That was even better.

"Oh yeah, ditto." Derek nodded enthusiastically, then let him in, closed the door, and backed him up against it. Closing the distance between them, Derek kissed him again.

He opened up and let Derek in, let Derek have him. Moaning, Derek pushed against him, pressing his back tight against the door as the kiss deepened. This wasn't playing video games....

He chuckled into Derek's lips, stretching up tall.

Derek grabbed his hips and slowly slid his hands up along Sawyer's sides, pushing his shirt up. Skin on skin, it was delicious.

"Hungry, hmm?" Sawyer's nipples drew up like they were trying to attract Derek.

"Uh-huh. I tried to be good." Derek tongue-fucked his mouth. "Tried to offer gaming." Taking his lower lip in, Derek sucked on it. "But not strong enough to resist you."

"That's not a bad thing." In fact, he found it heady.

"Oh good." Derek smiled around Sawyer's mouth before rubbing against him, body hard and sure as they moved together.

Someone had been thinking about him a lot at work. Damn.

Derek had gotten his hands as far as Sawyer's underarms, and he stretched his thumbs out, rubbing Sawyer's nipples, making the metal dig in and twist. The little ache made his eyes cross and shivers race across his body.

"Been thinking of touching you all day long. Wanna make you ache."

"Yes. Please." Sir.

Groaning, Derek slammed up against him and lifted him. He automatically wrapped his legs around Derek's waist so he was clinging like a limpet as Derek carried him to the bedroom, still kissing him.

"You're an addiction. I don't understand, but it's so good." Derek moaned the words against his skin.

Derek always managed to make him feel like the most wonderful, sexiest man alive. It was quite the gift.

Derek sat on the bed, hands wandering again, sliding over his body. "Mmm... you aren't naked. Why aren't you naked?"

"I was working."

"You're not working now," Derek pointed out. Like that made all the difference.

"No. No, my computer is in my apartment." Had he locked his door?

"Mmm." Derek rolled them, putting him on his back in the middle of the mattress, and ground down against him. Suddenly the state of his door didn't matter so much.

Derek's kisses danced over his face, wet and soft across his cheeks, his forehead, his nose and jaw.

Sawyer lifted his chin, offering his face for more of those kisses. There was something so needful, so necessary about them. It was crazy—he hadn't known Derek long enough for that to be true, yet it was.

And somehow it just got worse—better?—whatever. Bigger. It got bigger every day.

Derek tugged at his clothing, trying to work it open but clearly not willing to move away from him, to stop grinding their bodies together.

He didn't help. His hands were full of Derek's shoulders, fingertips digging in and rubbing hard.

He thought better of not helping for a half a second when the sound of material ripping preceded the sudden rush of air against his chest. But it was followed up by Derek's hands on his bare skin, and he didn't care. It was just a T-shirt.

Derek mapped him, hands dragging up and down, and his muscles rippled under the pressure. He pushed up into each touch, Derek playing him like he was a favorite instrument. He twisted and snuggled, fighting to get closer.

"Do you still have it in?" Derek asked, one hand tugging at his jeans.

"Yes. You didn't say I could take it out."

Derek shuddered. "Fuck, that's hot."

Derek flipped him over and tugged down his jeans, exposing his ass. Groaning, Derek bit his right asscheek.

Sawyer arched, drawing his legs up under him. Derek kissed and licked and bit at his skin, fingers digging in too as Derek held on to his asscheeks. Then Derek's thumb glanced across the base of the plug, bumped it, then pushed it.

"Oh God. Derek. Please." That ached so good.

"You want me to take it out?" Derek pushed at the base again, teasing him with it.

"I want you to do what you want to. I want you to decide."

Derek groaned. "I want to play with it. See how much I can make you moan and whimper from it."

Tugging on the base, Derek pulled it partway out. Sawyer felt his body resist, the plug having been seated so long. Derek had a good hold of the base, though, and kept tugging, insisting on maintaining control of the plug buried inside him.

He sucked in a deep breath, let himself center, focus. The playing continued, little movements that promised so much more.

"Making me a little crazy." Hell, a lot crazy.

"Good. Gonna up the ante. Make everything even bigger."

That worked for him. "Anything you want."

Derek hummed, sounding so pleased. He pulled the plug out, fucked Sawyer with it. The movements were rough, unpracticed, and that made them all the better.

His ass felt raw, open, like it was stretched wide. He pushed back, asking for more. Begging for it. Derek gave it to him, feeding him sensation after sensation, and nothing else in the world mattered.

"Jesus, you take it so well."

"I need. So much."

"Well, I love giving it to you." Derek's voice was thick with desire, happiness. Derek gave him a swat, nothing too heavy, just a nice crack across the flesh of his ass, making his butt jiggle, leaving a sweet tingle behind.

Derek rubbed, then swatted again, before fucking him a couple of times with the plug. Then before he could say anything, cool lube was pressed in alongside the plug, Derek's fingers adding to the stretch.

He cried out and spread his legs wider, his balls swinging between his thighs.

"It's good, yeah?" Derek added still more lube, making the glide of the plug superslick and almost cold for a moment along his hot flesh.

"Yeah. Yeah. God." His eyelids went heavy as his brain tried to process.

"Perfect." Derek slowed his movements, fucking him so slowly with the plug, twisting it at the same time. Every few thrusts, Derek would swat his ass, like a punctuation mark. It lit a fire under his skin, making him burn.

Derek clearly wasn't practiced, but he was enthusiastic and paid attention. When he found Sawyer's prostate with the end of the plug, Sawyer cried out loud, and Derek proceeded to shorten the length of his thrusts and hit that spot over and over again.

"Please!" The pleasure and pressure were huge and made him shudder.

"Please what?" Derek asked. "More of this?" He shoved the plug in hard. "Or more of this?" He swatted Sawyer's ass. "Or something else?"

"I don't know!" He shook, overwhelmed.

"Dealer's choice, then." Derek shoved the plug in deep and hard, then bit his asscheek again, teeth rough and sharp, so good.

God, he wanted to jack himself off, to tug his prick hard and fast and shoot into the blankets, but he knew better.

Derek seated the plug again, hands sliding up and down his thighs, moving to grab his hips now and then and bring him back into a new bite.

Sawyer let his body drop toward the sheet so he could start fucking the mattress. Derek tugged him back up, the strength in his hands wonderful. "Come back here, Sawyer."

"Yes, Sir," he moaned.

Derek groaned. "Gotta admit, I like the way that sounds." Derek swatted his ass a few more times, then bit where he'd swatted. "God, that's so pretty. You're amazing, Sawyer. Truly."

"I need you. I do. Please."

"Yeah, yeah. I need you too. So bad." Derek finally pulled the plug right out and didn't push it back in.

Sawyer wagged his ass like he was in heat, so empty, needing to be filled again.

Derek reached over him and grabbed a condom, the long body pressed up all along his. So hot, so strong. God.

He pushed up into Derek's strength with a low, happy cry. Derek rubbed against him, then slowly dragged down along his body as he moved back into place.

"Soon, baby. I promise."

"God, I'm empty. I ache for you."

"I'm right here." Derek snuggled up against his ass, cock hot and slick, pushing at his hole—a blunt battering ram.

He bore back, taking what he needed with a low groan. Derek pushed too, and that thick, lovely cock spread him open. It filled him so good—hot and right.

Sawyer curled his fingers in the bedsheets and clenched hard, trying to give Derek all the sensation he could.

"Oh God." Derek pushed in and in until his hips pressed hard against Sawyer's ass. Then he wriggled.

Sawyer bucked, pulling away before slamming back. Derek wrapped his fingers around Sawyer's hips and took over, dragging him back and slamming into him at the same time. It was so much better with Derek's strength added in. He loved how Derek's hips slapped against his ass, adding a little buzz.

"Fucking love this." Derek's fingers dug in tighter, pulling him back even harder.

"Yes. Yes, love it. Making me fly."

"Uh-huh." They slapped together again and again, like Derek was trying to climb into his body.

He took every inch, every bit of that thick, heavy cock.

"So hot," Derek nibbled on his neck, biting at his skin.

That sting made his eyes roll, and he thrust back, fucking himself.

"More! More!" Derek kept meeting him, ramming into him. The entire fucking bed was shaking.

He took and gave, making sure that he worked for Derek's orgasm.

Derek grabbed his cock, fingers wrapping tightly around it, and began jerking him off as they fucked. It was exactly what he needed, the pleasure shooting to his balls and up his spine.

"Soon!" he warned. "I can't...."

"Do it! Do it! Come on, baby—come for me." Each word came with a thrust, Derek slamming into him so hard.

His balls emptied, his world spinning like a top.

Derek shouted his name out and froze, buried deep inside him. He moaned softly, head on his folded arms.

"That was amazing."

"Ye—" Derek cleared his throat. "Yes, it was. Is." Derek kissed his neck, lips soothing where he'd bitten. Then Derek pulled out, leaving him so empty.

He tried not to cry out, but he couldn't help it.

"Shh. Shh." Derek continued to drop soft kisses on his back, lips warm, delicious. He dropped onto the bed next to Sawyer, kissed his arm this time.

"Sorry. So empty. I didn't mean to."

"Your poor ass needs a bit of a break." Derek patted his buttcheek.

"Yeah." Not really. He could take days of ass play.

Derek kissed him, tongue lingering. "You feeling less bleh?"

"Uh-huh. I'm feeling melty."

"Cool. Let's be melty together." Derek rubbed his nose against Sawyer's.

"Is that a song?" he teased. They snuggled together, and he found himself blinking slowly.

"It could be, eh? Let's get together. Let's melt together. Let's be me-e-el-el-ty!"

Sawyer chuckled softly, nuzzling into Derek's throat. Derek wrapped an arm around him, fingers sliding on his skin seemingly without any rhyme or reason. He could get used to this again. He really could.

"So, you used to do this kind of thing a lot, eh?"

"Yes. It was our life." He tried not to blush. "Is that weird to you?"

"No. It's what Luke and Benny do, and I sort of play along. Is that weird to you?"

"No. No, twenty-four/seven is rare."

"Is that what you were with your man? Twenty-four/seven? Is that what you're looking for now?"

"Those are two questions." He didn't want to answer the last one either, because he didn't know how to. "But yes, James and I were full-time."

"You didn't say anything till Luke sorta made you."

"I know that it's not… widely respected. I don't want to embarrass anyone."

"You don't embarrass me." Derek lifted his chin and looked into his eyes. "Sex isn't something to be embarrassed about."

"No, of course not." But this was about more than sex. This was about service and control and sex and pain and pleasure.

"I'm not practiced like Luke. I don't know all the things he does." There was obvious worry in Derek's eyes. Worry that he wouldn't be enough.

"I like Luke a lot. He's a great Dom, but you're…." He leaned in, nuzzled Derek's ears. "You're special."

"Oh…." Derek turned his face and kissed him hard. "I think you are too. I've kind of thought so since we first met."

"You showed me. I loved it. How kind and good you were to me."

Derek wrapped around him and held on tight. "I'm going to do everything I can to give you what you need."

"Mmm... ditto. Same for me." Oh, he felt like a million bucks.

"For now, I think that means snuggling, pizza, gaming, and more orgasms. Not necessarily in that order."

"Sounds like heaven, in any order." He kissed Derek's jaw, the "Sir" silent but meant.

Derek curled around him, kisses soft and lazy but deep nonetheless.

Sawyer sighed and let himself relax. He could get back to work later.

CHAPTER EIGHT

BENNY FINISHED work and headed home, a black cloud following him. He'd worked his ass off, including getting a piano up to the third floor. He was hot, sweaty, tired, and he needed an iced coffee as big as his head.

He went into the house and started for the stairs. As he passed Derek's door, he could hear voices and video game noises. Sounded like somebody—or at least two somebodies—had had a good day.

"Assholes," he grumped and stomped up the staircase to his apartment and the pitcher of iced coffee waiting for him to enjoy in a cold shower.

Luke's head popped out of his apartment before Benny could disappear into his. "Hey, Benny, my boy."

"Hey." He tried not to snarl because he wasn't mad at Luke.

"You look like you've had a bad day." Luke stepped back into his apartment, the door sliding the rest of the way open.

"Yeah. A shit one." He looked over with the faintest smile. "I was going to get caffeinated and wet."

"I've got water and coffee. Come inside, little boy." Luke gave him a wink before turning and heading deeper into his apartment.

"Little boy. Right." He went, though, didn't he?

He shut the door behind him, then followed Luke's ass all the way to the kitchen. Luke nodded at the chair, and he sat.

"You want hot or cold caffeine?"

"Cold. Please."

Luke opened the fridge and pulled out a can of Coke. He grabbed a glass, added ice, then poured the Coke into it and set it down in front of him.

"Thank you." He sucked it down, the icy bubbles so good they almost made him hurl.

Luke grabbed two more cans, poured one into a second glass of ice, then passed the other one over to him. "You are in a grumpyassed mood. I know how to fix that."

"It was just a hard day. Some of the guys were slacking, and it made things tough for the rest of us."

"And if you bitch about them, you're the grass, eh?" Luke came around behind him and began to rub his shoulders.

"Yeah...." Oh fuck. He melted, his body beginning to shake.

"You carry all your stress in your muscles. Are you sure that's all that's got you in a bad mood?"

He shrugged. "I guess so. Sure. What would I have to be bitchy about?"

"I don't know. You tell me, boy." Luke's fingers dug in deeper, insisting his muscles release the tension.

He didn't have any reasons. He was fine. Just fucking fine.

Luke dropped a kiss on the top of his head, then worked his shoulders even harder. A soft sob wanted to come out, and he fought it with all he had.

"Let go, boy." Luke practically growled the words out. "You're home now. And I'm telling you to fucking let go."

"Stop it...." The sob escaped, hiccupping from him.

"Unless you throw a 'master' on the end of that, you're cruising for a good, long spanking."

"Fuck off! I'm not like Sawyer. I'm not like the perfect sub."

Luke spun him around, chair and all, which was pretty damn impressive. "Watch how you speak to me, boy. And you're the perfect sub for me."

"I just wanted a shower!" He groaned, a sudden heat flooding his belly.

"A shower sounds great. You know I love shower sex." Luke laughed, the sound deep and happy. Luke scooped him up and dragged him into the bathroom like he weighed nothing at all.

He considered fighting but decided he would save his energy for once they were in the bathroom. Once there, he pulled out of Luke's hold, growling.

Luke only smiled.

"What are you grinning at?"

"You. I like your fire. I was missing it."

He frowned deeper, but inside he was incredibly pleased.

Luke grabbed him and tugged him close, mouth closing over his. He leaned into Luke's hands, wanting Luke to fight for it. Luke took hold of his chin and tilted his head, deepening the kiss, devouring his mouth, bruising him.

Yes.

Yes, that was what he needed.

Luke shoved him up against the wall, giving him no quarter, his head banging against the tile.

God, he needed this. He needed it so badly. He fought Luke, and Luke held him tight, knowing how to help.

Luke grabbed his arms and pressed them up against the wall above his head, pinning him in place.

"Don't make me punish you, boy."

"What if...?" What if he needed it?

"Then fight, boy. Fight with everything you have." Luke's hands tightened on his wrists.

He growled and let loose, tugging furiously at Luke's grip. Luke was too strong, though, grip holding. Benny's muscles were tired, worn down from a hard day's work.

He kept fighting, though, tiring himself out as his master gave him something to push against. He began to fade, his struggles becoming halfhearted.

"That's it, boy. I've got you." Luke pushed up against him, pressing him to the wall. The weight felt good covering him.

He moaned, the buzz of happiness starting to fill him. Humming into the kiss, Luke moved against him, crowding harder.

"Mmm... you've earned your punishments today, boy."

Benny moaned in protest, although he knew it was true.

"Gonna make you feel it all through the night. And you'll know in the morning who fucked you."

"I always know. Always."

"Well, I'm going to remind you." Luke took his mouth again, the kiss rough, harsh, and just what he needed.

He opened up, letting Luke devour him. He burned from balls to bones. Luke worked a leg between his, pressing up against his need. Then Luke skimmed off his shirt.

He bore down, rubbing on Luke hard enough that it ached.

"Make sure you don't come before the shower. Gonna love you so good. Give you what we need."

"I won't. I wasn't even horny."

"Maybe not—but you needed. And now you still need and you *are* horny."

"Yeah." He bore down again.

Luke grabbed one of his nipples and twisted, the zing going straight to his balls.

He arched up, needing more, sharper, harder.

Biting his bottom lip, Luke twisted his nipple again. "Shower, Benny. I need to do you up against the tile."

"Do you?" He whimpered, but he went to the shower.

"I totally fucking do." Luke stripped quickly, following him in and pushing him up against the far side of the stall. The tile was cold, shocking against his skin before Luke turned the water on and it splashed down around them. Then Luke spread his asscheeks wide, baring his hole.

Two slick fingers pushed at him, then into him, opening him up. He bucked back, taking them deep, and Luke put a hand across his lower back. "My pace."

He groaned, but Luke was intractable. Those fingers stayed inside him but didn't move, didn't move a fucking inch until he stilled. Then it started again, Luke pushing in hard, fingers pinging off his gland.

As soon as he moved, Luke stopped. Groaning, Benny rested his head against his hands where they lay on the tile. He squeezed his asscheeks tight, hoping that would encourage Luke to move. Luke didn't. Benny wasn't surprised—he knew how strong Luke was. How stubborn.

"You know how this goes, Benny."

"So fucking mean to me," he complained.

Luke burst out laughing. "Only you would call me opening you up on the way to fucking you mean."

He had to chuckle, had to. Luke did know how to make him smile.

"That's better." Luke licked at his neck, then dragged his tongue up along to Benny's earlobe.

"Mmm…," Benny sighed, the tension from the day easing.

Luke kept licking, sucking the water off his skin. He almost missed when two fingers became three. Almost. Luke added a twist to his thrust in, so Benny suddenly couldn't miss it.

He arched, his lips dropping open. "Luke!"

"Right here, boy." Luke found his gland, touching off it several times before twisting his fingers as he thrust again. Benny both loved and hated when Luke did this. It felt amazing but also drove him crazy, made him need more, or a rhythm or something. Anything.

"Mmm… needy boy. I know you want more, but I give you what you need, right?"

He nodded. He couldn't deny that.

"And sometimes I even give you what you want." Luke bit his earlobe, teeth sinking in before Luke grabbed it up between his lips and began to suck.

"Uhn." He arched and bucked, feet thrumming on the floor.

Luke worked his ass, opening him up in the most pleasurable way. "You're almost ready for me."

"I'm ready. I swear."

Luke slapped his butt. "Who decides that?"

He groaned again. "Master… please." He wanted Luke so damn badly. If he didn't get it soon, he was going to scream.

"Answer me, boy. Who owns your pleasure?"

"It's you, Luke! You do!" Fucker. He just wanted to get plowed good and hard.

He ignored the little voice that insisted it was more than that.

"That's right. I do." Luke pegged that spot inside him over and over, giving him no mercy.

Then Luke's fingers disappeared, leaving him empty. Even though he knew it wouldn't last very long, he mourned them. He hated being empty.

"You know it's coming."

"I know. I need it."

"I know that too. But making you wait for it? That makes it even better." Luke chuckled softly, but the sound was wicked as hell.

"Evil...." So perfectly, wonderfully evil.

"Master Evil to you, baby." Luke bit his right shoulder, lips wrapping around his skin. Luke began to suck.

A buzz filled him up, burning him deep inside.

Still sucking on his shoulder, Luke worked his cock between Benny's asscheeks and pressed hard against his hole. It was slow and sure, Luke's cock sinking into his body.

As soon as Luke was buried inside him, Luke found his nipples and began tugging, squeezing. He jerked and bucked between the sensations, his whole body alive and connected. Luke set a hard, fast pace, slamming into him, making sure to make his nipples throb with each thrust.

He shouted, screamed into the water falling around them.

Luke never stopped, sending him higher and higher.

Benny finally had to let go and breathe, to submit to Luke's will.

"That's it, Benny. Give yourself to me."

Luke always knew when it happened. Always.

He nodded. "All of me is yours."

"Yes!" Luke grabbed his cock, squeezed it, and began jacking him, sliding those amazing fingers up and down along his length. His orgasm began to build, his entire body tensing.

Luke grabbed his balls. "Don't you come before I say you can."

"Or what?" God, he loved this man.

"Or I'm going to spank you hard enough you won't be able to sit down for days." Luke's growl was sexy as hell, and the sound of it slid along Benny's spine. "I'll bind your pretty cock and balls and blister your hole with my crop. Then I'll make you tell Derek what you made me do."

He groaned and shook his head.

"And I'll get Sawyer to help. Have him twist in the biggest plug I've got." The promises in Luke's voice were sure.

"Shut up!" He bore down hard.

"Then stop trying to run the show, and don't come." Luke rubbed his thumb across the tip of Benny's cock, pressed in.

That burn wasn't fair—not at all.

"You just hold on, boy. Hold on until I say." Luke's thrusts were stronger now, pinging hard against his gland.

"Please. Please say. Pretty please," he begged.

"Hold on, Benny. You know I will let you come, but you need to hold on first."

He fought to obey, to be good, to give Luke what he asked for.

"Now, boy," growled Luke. "Give me your pleasure now."

The order was unexpected, coming so soon, but his body reacted without thought from him, spewing his pleasure out in a long shot, matched by Luke's gratification.

"Such a good boy. So obedient," Luke murmured, sounding a little melted.

"Fuck off."

Luke chuckled and rubbed his cheek against Benny's back. Luke's five-o'clock shadow scraped slightly on his skin.

"Uhn." That made him bare his teeth.

"You ready to move this to the bed, Benny? Or maybe you want to go downstairs and join Derek and Sawyer?"

"I want to stay up here." He wasn't ready to share.

"Oh, you have had a day, haven't you?" Luke turned off the water and handed him a towel. The two of them dried themselves off.

"Yes. Yes, I have. I feel... like everything is sore."

"Even your insides, hmm?" Luke pulled him in for another kiss.

Mainly his insides, he thought.

Luke dragged him to the bedroom, manhandling him like only Luke could. His fucking strong master.

He let Luke lead because he wanted to, because he needed to.

Luke tossed him onto the bed and went to the cupboard. "You need something stronger than me to fight against today."

"Huh?" He sat up, stared.

Luke tossed padded cuffs onto the bed next to him.

His belly went tight, and his prick jerked. "No." God, yes.

"Not your choice, boy. Not your choice at all." Luke cupped his jaw, rubbed against his lips.

Groaning, he pulled Luke's thumb into his mouth and sucked.

"Yeah. That's my sweet, slutty boy. I'm going to take such good care of you."

He sucked harder on Luke's thumb, biting the tip.

"Toothy!" Luke laughed, deep and low.

Fuck, this man made him feel good. Important.

Luke pushed his thumb deeper, fucking his lips with it, keeping his focus tight. "Time to get you all tied up."

He groaned, but Luke didn't seem to care. He straddled Benny's hips. "Hands up on the headboard, Benny."

His hands moved without his permission. Stupid hands. He gripped the headboard, squeezing it tight, making it creak and groan, and in seconds he was cuffed, his hands trapped.

He tugged, and Luke nodded. "That's right, boy. You test them as much as you want. You're not going anywhere."

"What are you going to do with me?"

"Whatever the fuck I want."

He stuck his tongue out at his lover.

Luke pounced, grabbing his tongue between quick fingers, and tugged. "*Tsk, tsk, tsk.* That's not very respectful."

Damn, that was impressive. He tried to pull his tongue away, but no dice.

"Next time you stick it out, I'm going to make you use it."

Like that was a hardship. He loved Luke's cock.

"Oh, you want this, do you?" Luke rolled against him, cock dragging along his belly, hot and hard, and he craved it.

"Always," he admitted. "Always want you."

"Good answer." Luke climbed him, hard cock coming ever closer.

"The truth." He loved Luke. Full stop.

"That's even better." Luke gazed down at him, teasing him with the tip of that hot cock sliding around his lips. He opened up, tongue lapping at the slit.

"Mmm. Yeah, do it right. I know you can."

He wrapped his lips around the crown of that thick cock and began to pull. Hard. Luke grunted, pushing partway in before pulling almost all the way out—making him work for it.

He tightened his lips, flicking the slit furiously.

"Fuck!" Luke shuddered above him, and that lovely slit began to leak. He pressed the tip of his tongue in, fucking it easily.

"Gonna make me come so fast." He could hear the truth of Luke's words in his tone.

Again? Impressive. That made him feel a hundred feet tall. And he worked even harder to make it happen, squeezing the head of Luke's cock between his lip-covered teeth.

"Damn, baby. I'm going to wear your ass out."

This first, though. He got to give Luke the blow job of his life. He could do this for Luke, and no one else could. He wanted to make sure Luke didn't decide the new guy was better at this.

Luke began to undulate, the thick cock sliding deep time and again, soft noises coming from Luke. For him. He made Luke make those noises.

Benny hummed, letting Luke feel him all the way along his shaft.

"Soon. Soon. Soon. Oh fuck." Luke's movements became harder, jerkier, sending the thick cock deep into his throat.

Yes. Yes, please. He yanked at the cuffs, sucking harder and harder.

Luke's shout was his warning, and suddenly Benny's mouth was full of come, the liquid sliding down his throat. He swallowed convulsively, taking it all in.

Luke rubbed both hands through his hair, then grabbed a handful and tugged his head back, slowly pulling out.

He licked his lips, whimpering softly. Luke patted his cheeks, then bent and brought their mouths together. "So good. You're like magic."

"Love," he whispered, just barely against Luke's lips.

"Mmm… yeah, baby." Luke settled next to him, fingers running idly over his skin. "Enjoying those cuffs? There's more where they came from."

"Uh-huh. Please. I want everything. Need it."

"Then I'm your man." Which Luke totally was.

Benny chuckled softly, rolled his head on his shoulders, and began to relax, his aching balls easing back. Luke had him. This day was going to end so much better than it had been going.

CHAPTER NINE

LUKE MADE breakfast, flipping the eggs carefully so he didn't break the yolks. He loved the weekends, especially when they started with Benny in his bed. Humming, he set the table.

He looked outside, surprised to see Sawyer out there hauling dirt and plants, the white T-shirt already streaked with sweat. He watched for a moment before going out onto the balcony. "Hey."

Sawyer looked up, waved. "Morning. Did I wake you? I was trying to be quiet."

"I was up. Making breakfast. You and Derek should join us."

"I haven't seen him today. I'm not sure he's awake."

"You guys didn't spend the night together?" Now that surprised him. He'd thought they were pretty tight. And if Derek wasn't in love, up was now down.

"I had a deadline. I haven't been to bed yet."

"Oh, you need a keeper." He was going to have to teach Derek how to help Sawyer with this kind of thing. Because really, Sawyer should be sleeping now if he was up all night.

"Enjoy your breakfast. I want to get this gardening done before it gets too hot."

"Sure. You and Derek should come up later. It'll be fun."

Sawyer waved and bent back to work, so Luke went to call Derek.

"'Lo?"

"Good morning. Do you know where your boy is?"

"Huh? My who?"

"Sawyer. You know he didn't sleep all night, right? And that now instead of sleeping he's out in the garden working like a sweaty, dirty maniac." If he didn't know that Sawyer needed a keeper, he wouldn't be pushing it, but everything about Sawyer begged for a master to help keep him on an even keel.

"Dude. That sounds like less than fun."

"Exactly. So maybe you should go do something about that, eh? Come on up later. We'll have lunch and other stuff."

Derek chuckled. "Okay."

"Okay. Talk to you later." He hung up and went to the window, grinning when he saw Derek, wearing nothing but a pair of boxer briefs, making his way over to Sawyer. Good deal.

He turned his attention back to breakfast. The eggs had now been cooking for way too long, so he tossed them and cracked some new ones into the pan. Then he moved the stuff on the table to a tray—Benny was clearly not going to be up anytime soon if he didn't go and help him out.

Benny was sleeping, plugged and pinked ass bare and up in the air like a target. It was more than he could resist. He set the tray down on the bedside table and took off his robe. He climbed onto the bed and swatted that fine bubble butt. Nice and hard. The swat rang out, his palm burning for a moment where it had connected with Benny's naked ass.

"Motherfucker!" Benny popped up like a jack-in-the-box.

"It's not your mother I'm interested in," he noted dryly. Then he rubbed Benny's ass before swatting it again. "When did you get such a foul mouth?"

"When you fucking started swatting before breakfast."

That made him chuckle, and he rubbed the lovely ass before bending to kiss one cheek, and then the other.

"Mmm. That's better."

"Hedonist." He rubbed some more. "You're going to have to sit on it to eat the breakfast I made you." He patted Benny's hip to get him moving.

"Oh, you spoil me, man. Thank you." Benny sat up gingerly and gave him a slow, burning kiss.

"All part of the package." He wasn't only into the spanking or whatever. He wanted the aftercare, the love, the spoiling, the being together.

Benny nuzzled his jaw. "Mmm. You want to feed each other?"

"I do. That's why I brought the food in." He dipped a corner of his toast into one of the egg yolks and then held it up to Benny's lips. "I made your favorite bacon—the sea salt and honey one."

"Oh… yum." That earned him another happy kiss. Someone was cheery this morning.

It was amazing what a little attention and a lot of love could do for a man. For this man.

He offered over a piece of bacon, along with another bit of yolk-dipped toast. Benny ate eagerly, then fed him a bite in return, taking care to make sure he got the best bits.

"You take good care of me, Benny." He rested his hand on Benny's thigh.

"You think so?" Benny searched his eyes.

He looked back at Benny, staring at him. "I know so. Why are you questioning that?"

"I'm not."

"No? You sure?" It had sounded like Benny was to him. He fed Benny another piece of bacon.

"God, I love that stuff. So good." Benny crunched away, and it made him laugh.

They'd have to work extra this weekend to keep their arteries from hardening, but he did love feeding his baby bacon.

They polished off breakfast, then went to do dishes together, as they had for years. Afterward, they returned to the bedroom, and he glanced out the window. Sawyer wasn't outside anymore. Good. Derek must have found something to occupy him with.

"Shall we go down and get the kid and his guy?"

"Do you like him?"

"You mean Sawyer?" Because Benny knew Derek and wasn't threatened by him.

"Yeah. He's…. He's a hard-core sub, huh?"

"He is." He knew Derek would move heaven and earth to try to give Sawyer what he needed. Kid was lucky he had someone to teach him the things he needed to know.

"Are you going to be his too, do you think? I know you like him. Are drawn to him."

"You don't think I'm master enough for both of you?"

"That's a trick question."

"I didn't mean it as one. Besides, I think Derek might have something to say about the matter."

Benny frowned at him. "I don't want you to replace me, but I'm not… I'm not as subby as him. I can tell. I could top him."

"Benny. I'm not looking for a replacement. No one could ever replace you. I like you just as you are. You're exactly what I want." He was doing something wrong if Benny wasn't confident in his place.

"He's just…." Benny sighed. "He's so pretty and perfect and nice. Like genuinely nice."

"Whereas you are a total brat who is ugly as sin and a total asshole." Luke snorted. "And that was sarcasm, boy. You are a brat, but I like that. You're perfect for me." He stroked Benny's back. "Does it wig you out? That you want to top him?"

"A little. It's weird."

"He'd let you." Luke wasn't sure it was what either Benny or Sawyer needed, but Sawyer would totally be willing. Benny was right—he was a genuinely nice man. Derek had picked a good man to fall for. "But I'm not sure Derek would let you."

"No? Derek's not real toppy. Or he hasn't been. He seems happy to be with you."

"That's because he's a happy, easy guy. And that's why he's going to learn how to be a Dom, because he's going to want to give Sawyer what Sawyer needs. But I think there's a possessive streak inside him he's not even aware of yet." Luke knew all about that possessive streak. He had it in spades when it came to Benny.

"Yeah?" Benny leaned against him. "It'll be fun, watching you teach Derek how to do this."

"You going to be nice?" Benny had a wicked streak that you had to get used to.

"Probably not, but I'll try." Benny winked at him, teasing playfully.

Luke laughed. As much as anything at Benny's honesty.

"So, what are they up to today? Derek and the sunshine boy?"

"I told them to join us later. I might have said we'd come down and get them."

"Ah. Okay. So, we should go?"

"We can finish our conversation. I want to know how you feel about there being four of us having benefits now."

"I don't know. I mean, it was super hot, but I didn't expect him to be, like, this professional sub. That's intimidating."

He did need to do work with Benny. His boy should know that he was his. "So are you planning to start behaving?" He was pretty sure the answer was no. He hoped the answer was no.

"Not really, no. I get off on pushing you."

"Good boy." He rolled over on top of Benny and gave him a kiss, controlling it, mastering his boy. He pushed his knee between Benny's legs, nudging the plug hard. He wanted his boy revved up, needing.

He pinched one nipple, then the other, loving the way those little bits of flesh hardened for him. He rolled them, then leaned forward to bite one tight bud, hard.

"Fuck!"

"Yeah, that's coming." One kiss melted into another. "First we're going to head downstairs and give our good friends a lesson, hmm? After your nips are aching and swollen?"

"No...."

"Yeah. I want to be able to make them ache just looking at them." He pinched again, twisting the right one harder than the left. He'd never had these pierced because he could spend hours biting and pinching them. Some days he made Benny come without ever touching his cock.

Benny arched for him, offering him one low moan after another. Every time he pinched, Benny would buck.

"Stop. No more."

He chuckled. "You don't really want it to stop, do you?"

Benny glared at him.

He chuckled and pinched harder. "I could use my teeth, boy."

"No more. They burn."

That was his cue. He leaned in and used his teeth, biting gently at first, but then with more force.

Benny was leaking hard beneath him, ass working the plug in time with his bites.

"No coming from this. Not now. I want you hard and needing when we go see Derek and Sawyer."

"Master! You can't...."

"Of course I can. I am." He used his thumb to pinch his nail over the right nipple, working it. "What should we teach Derek today, my love?"

Benny's answer was a moan, then a quiet "How to beat you for doing my nipples?"

"It gets me off, seeing them swollen and hard, red and stiff. Don't you want me staring at you?"

"You cheat...."

He grinned. "There is no cheating in BDSM. What if we get you super tender, then challenge Derek to make Sawyer's match?"

Benny's eyes lit up. "Oh, that would be so cruel. So hot."

Leaning in, he took one of Benny's nipples in and sucked hard, pulling the flesh away from Benny's chest. He pressed the swollen nub against the back of his teeth with his tongue, pulling rhythmically. Benny's hands were holding his head, his boy crying out again and again.

He flicked his tongue back and forth across the tip of Benny's nipple as he rubbed his teeth along the rest of it.

"Please, Master. Please, I need to come."

"No. I said you couldn't." He growled and moved to Benny's other nipple, blew on it before taking it into his mouth. He bit and sucked, tugging hard with his teeth as he pinched and rolled the one he'd just finished with. He wanted to challenge Derek and Sawyer as much as he wanted to challenge his boy.

He rubbed the nipple not in his mouth with his thumb, pressing it in. The skin was hot, swollen, begging for his attention. He gave it, working both nipples like he was getting paid for it.

"I'm going to shoot. Master. Please. I can't hold on."

"Good boy for telling me." Benny was trying hard, he could tell.

He rummaged through his side table drawer and came up with a leather cock ring. He didn't tease, not if Benny was close—another day he might want to push Benny into a punishment, but today he wanted that cock needy when they joined Derek and Sawyer. Benny keened softly as he was ringed, then began to pant.

"Thank you. Thank you."

"Can you take more, boy?"

"Yes, Master. Yes. More."

He did love it when Benny embraced his need and begged for it. He kept going, twisting the swollen flesh now as he abused it.

Benny watched, eyes heavy-lidded as the sweet tits pressed into Luke's fingers. He kept going, and Benny became restless, unable to remain still the longer he stayed on the hot flesh.

Once the flesh was dark and bruised and swollen so desperately that the touch of air would make them throb, he decided they were ready. "Come on, boy. Let's go give Derek his first lesson."

"I don't think I can wear a shirt, Master."

"Mmm…. No. I think I want to be able to keep them hard." He reached out and rolled Benny's bound cock and balls, making his boy whimper.

Nodding, he got up. "You're ready."

"Sweats?" Benny asked.

He grabbed a pair of Benny's sweats, kept on hand for just such an occasion. He tossed them at Benny and grabbed his own, along with a T-shirt. Then they headed downstairs, both of them hard and aching, both of them ready to play.

Luke looked at both doors, pondering, then knocked on Sawyer's.

Derek opened the door, bare naked. "Hey. I'm trying to convince Sawyer to take a nap."

Luke chuckled. "I'm here to help."

"I'm here to make sure the two of you blow his mind." Benny gave Derek that wicked grin of his.

Derek stood back, inviting them in.

Sawyer was curled up on the sofa, lips kiss-swollen and parted. These two did like their kisses. It was sweet. Luke wasn't sweet—they needed him.

"You want to play out here or in the bedroom?" Sawyer had a good setup—decadent, the furniture good to play on. He didn't think Sawyer had necessarily chosen it that way on purpose, but subconsciously the guy had known exactly what he needed.

"Play?" Derek asked, eyes wide. "Luke?"

"You use him hard and he'll fall right asleep for you. Sawyer needs a lot, but he's not going to ask for it. Not yet. You need to be proactive. I told you I'd teach you. Now is your first lesson."

"But… are you sure?" Derek glanced at Benny, humming softly. "You've been busy."

"Uh-huh. I'm going to guide you to making Sawyer's nips match Benny's."

Sawyer's gasp was soft, but the need in it was audible as Sawyer's eyes sought out the dark, swollen, aching nubs on Benny's chest.

Luke stood behind Derek. "Look at the need in his eyes, Derek. Pay attention to his body—it will tell you what he needs, what he wants."

"What do you want me to do?"

"Get him naked and in bed," Luke whispered in Derek's ear. "He'll go sound to sleep once you're done."

Derek went to Sawyer and held out his hands. "Come with me, babe."

Sawyer didn't hesitate, hands sliding into Derek's, letting Derek pull him up and lead him down the hall. Luke and Benny followed.

Derek pulled Sawyer's shirt off, eased down the loose shorts. Sawyer clung to him, moaning when Derek brought their mouths together.

Luke wanted to moan too, the kisses they shared hot as hell to watch, but he had a job to do, a lesson to teach. They were going to have so much fun together.

"I want you to look at Benny's nipples, Derek. I want you to make Sawyer's as hard, as dark, as swollen."

"Do they hurt?" Derek asked, directing the question at Benny.

"They throb. I want to come, so bad."

Luke chuckled and swatted Benny's ass. "Take off those sweats, boy. Let Derek and Sawyer see how badly you need."

Derek moaned at the sight of Benny's package. "Oh yum." Derek reached out and cupped Benny's cock.

Benny hissed and humped Derek's hand. Derek didn't let go, but he shook his head.

"I don't think you're allowed to do that, are you?"

Luke grinned—the kid had damn good instincts. "No, he's not."

"He touched!" Benny groaned, and Derek chuckled softly.

"I'm allowed to touch. You aren't allowed to try to come." Derek was a quick learner. He was, however, focused on the wrong man.

"You're falling down on your task, Derek. Sawyer's nipples. Focus."

"His are pierced."

"They still bruise, honey."

Derek's eyes went wide, but he turned to Sawyer. "I'm gonna make your nipples look like Benny's. Only prettier, thanks to the jewelry." Derek climbed onto the bed and bent to Sawyer's nipples.

Sawyer gasped, wide-eyed, staring over at them in a delicious shock.

Luke gave him a smile and sat on the end of the bed, bringing Benny down with him so they could watch comfortably.

Derek bent to Sawyer's right nipple, taking it into his mouth.

"Suck it first, Dee, and get it hard. You'll need to start slow on the biting."

Sawyer groaned and bucked at the word biting. Then he bucked again as Derek began sucking.

"Hands up, Sawyer. Above your head for your master."

Sawyer whimpered softly, hands moving to clasp behind his head.

Derek groaned, fingers sliding along the insides of Sawyer's arms. Good. The kid was turned on by that. Next time he'd have to give the order himself.

Luke nudged Derek.

"Good boy," Derek said.

Luke grinned and resisted saying the same thing.

Sawyer smiled, the look gentle. "Thank you... Sir?"

Derek smiled back. "Do you think I've earned that? I don't want you to call me that if it's not time yet."

Sawyer looked worried, but he nodded, hands staying still.

"I like the way it sounds. And I want to learn for you."

"I'm here. I'll teach you." Luke would make sure Derek learned what he needed to do right by Sawyer. Because he didn't think Sawyer would be able to do without a master for the rest of his life.

Sawyer needed beautifully, and Derek would thrive having a sub to care for, to dominate.

He patted Derek's ass in encouragement.

Derek hummed and kept working Sawyer's nipples. He sucked on one and pinched and twisted the other one. Luke could see the little nubs, all hard and growing pinker. They'd be bruised and swollen soon.

He drew Benny closer to him, settling him so that he could stroke and tug too, keep his boy revved up. Benny groaned and rubbed back against him.

Sawyer began to undulate beneath Derek, moaning and whimpering as Derek worked his nipples.

"You can start to use your teeth, Dee."

Sawyer keened suddenly, telling Luke that Derek was following instructions.

"Start with just rubbing your teeth along the bud, over and over." He was hard as a rock, this lesson turning him on.

Derek moaned and did as he suggested, Sawyer humping the air pretty solidly. The sounds that came out of his mouth spoke of pleasure and need.

"Don't shoot, Sawyer," Derek whispered.

"Yes, S...."

Derek pulled back and looked up at Sawyer. "Yes...?"

"You said not to call you Sir."

"Oh. Yeah. If you didn't think I'd earned it yet. I guess I was hoping I had." Derek shrugged casually.

"I didn't want to offend you...." Sawyer flushed, shrinking away from Derek. "I'm just tired, I think."

"No! It's okay. I probably haven't actually earned it yet. Come back here."

Poor Sawyer was used to orders, while Derek was used to his lovers having options.

"You could be my Sir, if you wanted to."

"I do. I want to be everything you need."

"Then yes, Sir."

"See? So sweet," Benny whispered to Luke.

"Uh-huh. Sweet as pie." He rubbed his chin along Benny's shoulder, then placed a kiss there.

Meanwhile, Derek had gone back to working Sawyer's nipples. Sawyer's eyelids went heavy, soft moans splitting the air.

Luke stroked Derek's back, encouraging him to go on. Derek was doing a great job. "You're a natural, Dee."

Derek moaned, and whatever he did made Sawyer cry out. It made Luke moan, and he tweaked Benny's left nipple, then tugged on the right.

Benny arched, biting out a soft cry. "Master!"

He smiled against Benny's skin as Derek redoubled his efforts on Sawyer's nipples. The color was coming up nicely.

"Go lie next to Sawyer, boy, so we can compare color."

Benny groaned but moved away from him, lying down beside Sawyer as ordered.

Sawyer looked over at Benny, smiled. "Hey. I…. You look amazing."

Benny blushed but gave Sawyer a grin. "Thanks. I'm on fire."

"The color's not right yet," Derek noted, looking from Benny's chest to Sawyer's. He grabbed one of Sawyer's nipple rings and tugged on it, slowly drawing it from Sawyer's chest.

Sawyer arched, lips opened as he fought to ease the pressure. Derek didn't back off; instead he drew the other ring between his teeth and pulled at it as well.

"You can't resist him, boy," Luke told Sawyer. "He's your master."

Derek moaned at his words. Letting go of the rings, Derek went back to stimulating Sawyer's nipples directly.

Luke leaned over, whispering softly, "You're his master, he's your boy."

Derek moaned again, hips grinding against Sawyer's.

"Bite harder, Dee. Let him feel you now."

Sawyer cried out and bucked, fingers going white on the headboard as Sawyer gripped it tighter. Luke bent to Benny's little nips, giving his boy a reason to moan, a reason to cry out himself.

"Master!" Benny's hands landed on his head, fingers opening and closing in his hair like his boy couldn't decide whether to hold him closer or push him away. He sucked harder, closing his eyes and sinking into the pleasure.

The heat poured off the four of them, the scent of sex and pleasure rising on the air. He rubbed against Benny, feeling his boy's prick leaking against him.

He bet Sawyer was as bad, dripping and slicking their bodies. Derek rubbed his cheek against Sawyer's nipples, then kissed him.

"Let's compare again," Luke suggested.

Derek leaned back. Sawyer's nips were a deep, dark red, the rings standing from the flesh. They were a great match for Benny's, which were the same dark, needy color.

"I'm going to keep playing with them, and I want you to come just from that." Derek was trusting his instincts, and it seemed they were right on.

"Yes, Sir. I'll do my best."

Derek went back to torturing Sawyer's nipples, his body driving them together.

Luke could have told Derek that with all the stimulation in the lower regions, Sawyer totally wasn't coming just from the nipple stimulation, but he wasn't an ass, so he didn't.

Derek would learn when to back away, when to make Sawyer beg. Little steps.

Benny groaned and bucked up against him, rubbing.

"Needy slut," he teased. "Mine."

"Yes, Master. Please."

"Please what, boy?"

"Love me."

"That's the easiest thing in the world, Benny." He bit gently at Benny's throat, then wrapped his lips around one swollen nipple, flapping his tongue across the tip and sucking on the ubersensitive flesh. Benny bucked for him, his low roar filling the room. Lifting his head, Luke gave Benny a wicked grin. "You'll come just from this as well."

"No fair...." Benny arched into his touches. "I have the ring on."

"If I take the ring off, you'll have an unfair advantage over Sawyer. You'll come as soon as I do."

"Mean to me.... Derek's humping him dry."

"You telling me you want to come right away, or you want to wait a few minutes and let the anticipation and need build?" He knew his boy, knew Benny loved the anticipation, the ache. "I'll take it off when I'm ready. But if you happen to come anyway with the ring on, just from the nipple stimulation, then you can. No repercussions."

"Oh…," Benny moaned softly. "Yes, Master. Cool."

Sawyer looked at Benny with a smile, and Benny swooped over and kissed Sawyer hard.

Luke took the opportunity to grab Derek's head and pull him into a kiss as well. Derek always was a good kisser, but he seemed even more so now, like the extra time kissing Sawyer had improved Derek's technique.

Derek groaned into his mouth and pressed their chests together for a moment. Then all of Derek's attention was back on Sawyer and those poor pierced nips. Derek was going to town on them.

"Good job, Dee."

Sawyer bucked up, and Derek put one hand on Sawyer's hip. "Only from this. Do you understand?"

"Y-yes, Sir."

"Good boy." Derek pounced on Sawyer's mouth, taking it hard.

Luke and Benny both groaned. There was something hot about all that new passion. Derek and Sawyer both wore it well.

Derek broke the kiss, going back to working Sawyer's nips with mouth and fingers, and Luke was pretty sure it wasn't going to be a lot longer before Sawyer gave it up.

He bent to his own boy, finding a strong, steady suction that was meant to make Benny dizzy.

Both Sawyer and Benny were making the best sounds. Luke hummed around Benny's nipple, letting his noise add vibrations to the sensations he was giving Benny.

"Please. Please, love. Need." Benny was as vocal as Sawyer was quiet. His boy rocked down against the plug, fucking himself. It was a beautiful thing.

Sawyer suddenly cried out, bucking hard, and the smell of spunk filled the air.

"Sawyer!" Derek froze, and the smell got stronger.

"Master…." Benny bucked against him. "Please. Please, don't leave me out."

"We'll come together." He reached between them, bumping Benny's balls as he worked the ring off his boy. Like he'd leave his boy out, ever.

Benny cried out as soon as the ring was unfastened, cheeks turning bright red.

"Beautiful boy." As soon as he felt Benny's come between them, he drove himself against his boy and added his own pleasure to the mix. Orgasms were always better shared.

Benny curled into him, panting hard, and when he looked over, he found Sawyer already asleep.

Derek gave him a lazy smile. "Thanks, dude."

Luke chuckled. "Anytime."

Really, anytime at all. He was enjoying having a brand-new Dom, a bratty sub, and a really subby sub under him.

CHAPTER TEN

DEREK CAME home from work and popped a can of Coke, downing half of it in one go. Testing ice cream flavors was thirsty work, and he'd had more than his share of water already today. He grabbed a few cookies and changed into jeans and a new T-shirt with "Contents May be Larger than They Appear" written across it.

He checked his watch and smiled. He could totally go over to Sawyer's place and see if he was awake and had done enough work to take a break. He'd learned sometimes Sawyer worked at odd hours. Something about the flow of creativity.

He went across the hall and knocked. He could take Sawyer out to dinner. Or have him over for pizza. Or let Sawyer make them dinner. He kept saying he wanted to, but they kept getting distracted.

It made him smile. Hell, everything about Sawyer made him smile.

"Come in."

He opened the door and the smell of garlic and onions and tomatoes flooded his nose.

"Oh, wow. It smells amazing in here." He went to the kitchen to find Sawyer.

"Hey there! I thought I'd cook supper—spaghetti and meatballs with a Caesar salad and garlic bread. I didn't make dessert because you've had a ton of sweet already, though."

"I can have you for dessert." He drew Sawyer into his arms and took his mouth, tongue slipping between Sawyer's lips. Sawyer tasted like garlic. "You've been snacking."

"I have. I got the week's work done, so I've been playing."

His ears perked up at that. "So you're free for a while?" Because playing with Sawyer was so much better than working.

"I am. Until Monday. That's four days off."

"Oh, the fun we can have in four days."

Sawyer's eyes twinkled, crinkling at the edges. "Do you have thoughts?"

"I have a lot of thoughts. Do you have any?"

"To feed you and make you happy." Sawyer licked the corner of his lips.

"You make me happy just by being you." He chased Sawyer's tongue with his lips. He had some ideas about how he could make Sawyer happy. He'd been looking things up on the internet.

Between that and digging through books that Luke had—which oh my God—he was feeling… educated.

"How long until supper?" Was there time to fool around? Or just neck, even? Or they could talk. That was a novel idea. Honestly, he just wanted to spend time with Sawyer.

"Forty-five minutes, give or take. Maybe an hour."

"So we could sit and… talk or something?" He grabbed hold of Sawyer's ass and squeezed. Such a perfect handful.

"I know how to do that. Come sit on the sofa?"

"Yeah." They went together, and he sat, pulling Sawyer into his body, arm around Sawyer's shoulders. "How was your day?"

"Quiet. Easy. How about you?"

"I came up with a new flavor today. One that I think is going to stick. I may get a bonus."

"Yeah? What flavor is that?" Sawyer leaned into him with a soft sigh.

"Salted caramel with chunks of toffee. It's stunning."

"Uhn. Yes, please." Oh, that made him feel good.

"I'll bring some home once they've done a test run." There was always ice cream in his freezer. And Luke's and Benny's freezers too. "What's your favorite food?"

"French fries. I love fried foods, even though they're bad for me. I used to—" He cut off, then grinned. "Is yours ice cream?"

"Oh, I love ice cream, but my favorite ever food is peanut butter and jam sandwiches."

"Good to know. I'll keep them around for you."

"There's nothing better when you're feeling glum." He stroked Sawyer, pushing his hair behind his ear. "I'll make you french fries anytime you want."

"Thank you. I appreciate it." Sawyer kissed his cheek. "Do you have plans for the weekend?"

"I do. They involve rope and cuffs and nipple clamps, your bed, and you." He waited, hoping he'd gotten it right.

Sawyer gasped softly, the sweet man searching his eyes, lips swollen and parted. It looked like he'd done well.

"I'm going to blow your mind." Or die trying.

"Yes, Sir." Sawyer blinked at him, licked his lips.

He leaned in and followed Sawyer's tongue with his own. "We'll start after supper." Sawyer had worked hard to make him a meal. Besides, it smelled amazing, and his stomach was growling.

"Sounds wonderful. I hope you enjoy your supper."

"Based on the smell, I'd say I will. Did you say there's garlic bread too?" He had a spot in his stomach for garlic bread.

"Yes, Sir. Salad, spaghetti, meatballs, and garlic toast."

Derek had to admit, he did like how the "sir" sounded. It warmed him low in his belly and in his balls. "Sounds amazing. I feel like I'm going to a restaurant." They rarely did all the fixings like that, and since they each contributed, it was never all laid out for him like that.

"Except that you don't have to drive or tip your waiter," Sawyer teased.

"And I can kiss the cook." Tickled, he leaned in and did exactly that, pressing his lips against Sawyer's. Warm and supple, Sawyer's lips were still like heaven against his. He hoped this never faded, that kissing Sawyer always felt like magic.

Sawyer rested his hands on Derek's chest, then slowly slid them up and over. Joining his fingers behind Derek's back, Sawyer held on. Derek cupped Sawyer's cheek and tilted his head so he could deepen the kiss.

Sawyer opened for him without hesitation.

Sawyer slid on his lap, and he could feel the end of a plug, seated in that sweet, tight hole.

It made him gasp, and his hands dropped down, touched that sweet ass. He slid his fingers across the plug and groaned, frustrated by the clothing between his and Sawyer's skin.

"Did you do this?" From everything he read, Sawyer shouldn't have. Except that he hadn't forbidden it, so really, it was okay. He thought he should start forbidding stuff like that, though. If Sawyer needed a plug or an orgasm, Derek would provide it. All Sawyer had to do was ask. "Did you?" he asked again.

"Yes, Sir. I was aching for you." Sawyer looked up at him, blinking through his lashes.

That made him moan, and he licked his lips. "You should come to me if you need me. Ask for my help."

"Should I?" Sawyer rocked again. "I was empty, needing."

He touched his fingers to the base of the plug and pushed. "Next time that happens, you tell me. You have my phone number if I'm not home."

"Yes, Sir. Master. I will," Sawyer whispered to him. "I wanted to make myself come, wanted to ride the plug until I shot, but I put a ring on, made myself wait."

"That's good." Derek took a deep breath. "I don't want you to come without my permission anymore. Not even if Luke says it's okay. Your orgasms belong to me." That had been one chapter in Luke's books that had turned him on so much.

Sawyer offered him a low cry, and the rubbing increased. "Yes, Master."

He moaned again. Master made him even hotter than Sir. "No coming now until I say you're allowed to." And they were going to at least get naked before that happened. Sawyer's soft moan said he'd heard Derek's words, but Derek waited for the soft "Yes, Master" before saying, "Take off your shirt for me."

"Yes, Master." Sawyer stripped off the shirt, revealing his pierced nipples—not swollen anymore, barely pink.

Derek leaned in, mouth open, and wrapped his lips around the left nipple. He sucked on it, letting his tongue play with the piercing.

Sawyer moaned, body jerking hard. Yes! Derek flapped at the ring, flipping it up and down as he continued to suck. Then he grabbed the other piercing between his fingers, tugging lightly, then twisting it. The metal was hot from Sawyer's skin.

He groaned around Sawyer's nipple, eyes closing as he sucked. He loved the salt of Sawyer's skin, the sound of the deep, low moans.

He moved from the right nipple to the left, his fingers sliding across the right nipple as he sucked, feeling the heat and the wet from his mouth.

Sawyer drove against his thigh, rocking hard, a dark spot forming on Sawyer's slacks. So hot. Sawyer was the sexiest man he'd ever seen.

He grabbed Sawyer's ass again, squeezing, making sure his fingertips pushed at the base of the plug. He wanted to nudge Sawyer's gland with it.

"Is it big?"

"Yes, Sir. The big one that's shaped like a bullet."

He groaned. "That's pretty big." Almost as big as he was, really. "I want to see. Take your pants off."

Sawyer stood, slowly unfastening his slacks and letting them fall. The stiff plug was wide all the way down until the neck, which was tiny. It meant that Sawyer couldn't lose it while he cooked, and Derek would get to work to get it out of his boy.

"Turn around and bend over." Sawyer did, and he reached out, touching the little end of the plug. He pushed a few times, watching it almost disappear. "Remember, you ask me next time. Your pleasure, your need, is all mine."

Sawyer moaned, and his toes curled. It made Derek feel powerful and sexy. He worked his fingers around the base, barely grabbing on to it, and tugged gently. Nothing seemed to happen, so he tugged harder. He watched as Sawyer's tiny ring began to stretch, to bulge around the swelling of the plug.

He pressed his face against one asscheek and licked at the stretched edge of Sawyer's hole.

Sawyer's cry rang out, the sound wild and fierce. "Master!"

Oh yeah. He liked the way that sounded and wanted to get used to it. He kept licking, working his way slowly all the way around Sawyer's hole.

"Yours," Sawyer whispered to him. "Yours. I ache."

Yeah, yeah, that was right. Sawyer was his. He pulled the plug out a little more and turned it in a circle. The noises that Sawyer made had him so hard.

He glanced at the timer on the microwave. Fifteen minutes. That was enough time to make Sawyer insane, he thought.

He pushed the plug back in, then tugged it partway out again, rocking the plug back and forth. Every sound that Sawyer made drove him higher. He started leaking, dripping clear precome, slicking his thighs.

He tugged a little harder, bringing the plug almost all the way out, then pushed it back in just to hear Sawyer cry out for him.

"I read about things, Sawyer, about scenes we can play," he murmured. "We have four whole days."

He could blow Sawyer's mind over and over for four days. Four.

He finally tugged the plug right out. He swore Sawyer's hole snapped closed.

"Master!" Sawyer cried out and stood up, stumbling forward a few steps.

He wrapped his hands around Sawyer's hips, steadying him. "Easy. Easy. You're gonna come back here and ride my cock." Soon as he got undressed. "You go get the condom while I strip."

"Let me rescue the meatballs?"

"Uh-huh. Don't be long. I need you." He needed Sawyer so bad.

"I'll put them on really low to keep warm." Sawyer headed to the kitchen, that sweet ass right there and waiting for him.

He watched Sawyer moving as he removed his own clothing. He tossed his T-shirt and his jeans at the chair at the end of the couch. He never took his eyes off Sawyer the entire time.

Sawyer fiddled with the oven, then went to get a condom and lube from the bedroom. Derek licked his lips and shook himself. He needed to have control here—he couldn't lose himself in Sawyer's body, though it would be so very easy.

He took a few deep breaths. He needed to make Sawyer need, make him wild, and then make him wait for supper.

Sawyer came back, and he made grabby hands. Look at that beautiful man with the nipple rings in the swollen nips and his cock standing straight up and shining with precome.

Sawyer handed him the supplies. "Where do you want me, Master?"

"I want you to put the condom on me, and then I want you in my lap, riding me."

"Yes, Sir." Sawyer knelt gracefully, moving to cover his cock.

He whimpered as Sawyer's fingers touched his cock and bit his bottom lip. He wasn't ready to come yet. Not until he was buried inside of Sawyer's ass.

"Beautiful lover." Sawyer kissed the tip of his cock.

"You're the beautiful one." His voice cracked, but he managed to get the words out. Sawyer blew his mind.

"Thank you. I want to be beautiful for you."

"You are."

Sawyer's finger slid along his cock a couple more times, spreading lube on him. After only a few strokes, he wrapped his fingers around Sawyer's. "I need you to ride now."

"Yes, Master."

"You can't come, boy."

"I won't. I swear, Master. I won't."

"Even if I take the ring off?" Did Sawyer have that kind of control?

Sawyer nodded. "That will make it harder, but I can."

"Good. I like how your prick looks with it on, but it's even better with it off." He slid his finger along Sawyer's cock, right to the ring. He tugged at the snap, opening the leather.

The sweet prick immediately got harder, balls drawing up.

"I will have to punish you if you come, love."

Sawyer drew in a quick breath, but he nodded. "Yes, Master, I understand."

Derek wrapped his fingers around Sawyer's hips and drew him closer. Sawyer rubbed against the tip of his prick, once, twice, then sank down, taking him in with a single downward slide.

"Oh fuck!" He closed his eyes and took a few breaths. He was not going to come. Not until Sawyer had a wonderful ride.

"Master...," Sawyer moaned softly. "So big inside me."

"And you're so tight. Feel so good around me." He kept his fingers around Sawyer's hips, but really, for now at least, it was all Sawyer's show. Sawyer began to ride, moving up and down, driving himself all the way to the root.

Wanting a kiss, he brought their mouths together again, and they shared breath and. Sawyer bounced on his cock, little sounds escaping him, pushing into their kiss.

He wanted it to last forever, but Sawyer was so tight and was bouncing so quickly, squeezing Derek's cock and making it impossible to do anything but fly with this beautiful man.

Sawyer arched down, moving faster, harder, cock slapping against Derek's belly.

"You're going to come like this. Without me even touching your cock. And we're going to come together." And it was going to be soon because good fucking God, this was amazing.

"Master? Is that an order?"

"Yes, Sawyer. It is."

"Oh...." Sawyer beamed at him, body tightening around his cock like a fist. "Thank you."

He gazed at Sawyer's ecstatic face and realized suddenly how much Sawyer wanted the orders. No, craved them, needed them deep inside his soul.

He tightened his hands around Sawyer's hips. "When I say."

"Yes, Master. Thank you for letting me come. Thank you."

"It's my pleasure, boy." He tried the word out in his mouth. It felt a little strange, honestly. Sawyer was older than him. Maybe they would find their own word for it.

Sawyer clenched down, making him gasp and drive up into that tight sheath. He met every drop down after that, bucking up into his lover.

Meeting Sawyer's eyes, he made the call, his balls aching to let loose. "Now, Sawyer—come now."

He loved the way Sawyer's eyes went wide, expression needy and wanton, and then seed poured from his boy in thick ropes. Sawyer's body bore down on him, tighter than ever, and it had him crying out and filling the condom with his seed.

Sawyer snuggled into the curve of his throat. "Master."

Letting go of Sawyer's hips, he wrapped his arms around Sawyer's back and held on. "Sawyer." He kissed the top of Sawyer's head. Then he grabbed the throw off the back of the couch and wrapped it around them both.

"I should finish your supper, hmm?"

"It smells amazing. I can't wait to eat." He tilted Sawyer's head and took a long kiss. "Make sure you put an apron on so you don't burn anything important."

"Can you plug me again, Master? One day, maybe you can plug me full of your seed?"

Oh God. He thought he might short out there for a second, but he took a few breaths and managed not to. "You want to be exclusive? Because I'd love that. You are... really special. I knew it the moment I saw you." It was true. Maybe not love at first sight, but certainly strong like and definite lust, and now he was totally in love.

"Would that work with your friends?"

"We should all get tested." He wasn't going to risk Sawyer. Not for anything. "Nobody else gets to come inside you, though. Just me." He loved Luke and Benny; they'd been playing for long enough that it was more than just playing. But Sawyer was his. "You're mine."

"Oh. Oh, yes. Yes, Master. Please. Yes." Sawyer whimpered softly, beginning to move on his covered cock again.

He brought their mouths together once more, kissing hard as Sawyer rocked. He knew he probably should change out the condom, but he couldn't bring himself to make Sawyer stop. Not when there wasn't another one handy. "Needy."

"Yes. I love ass play. Love it."

"I'll remember that," he promised.

"What turns you on, Sir?"

"Everything." He thought sex was amazing. Especially with Sawyer. "You."

"Do you want to use me? Take me at will?"

God, Sawyer was a seductive little slut.

"Uh-huh. Like all the time." He would tie Sawyer to the bed and never let him go if real life didn't exist.

"I was made for this. I swear. I was made to serve."

"And I was made for you."

"Such a sweet man." Sawyer kissed him again, slowly, still riding him steadily.

He wrapped his arms around Sawyer and reclined against the back of the couch, bringing Sawyer with him so their bodies rubbed from shoulder to upper thighs. He wrapped his hands around Sawyer's waist, helping him move, helping him ride.

"You're delicious," he told Sawyer. "Truly."

"Thank you. Thank you so much." Sawyer's cock was still hard, rubbing against his stomach, leaving wet trails.

Reaching around, Derek rubbed his fingers along the place where they were joined. Fuck, it was hot. In all senses of the word. When he touched, Sawyer jerked forward with a soft cry, tongue flicking out.

He pushed one of his fingers into Sawyer alongside his cock, giving him extra girth.

The effect on his lover was stunning, a bright flush clawing its way up Sawyer's belly. Following that lead, he pushed in a finger from his other hand too. Then he slowly tugged his fingers apart and a spurt of seed shot from his lover.

He leaned their foreheads together, then took another soft kiss. "I've got to come out now. You clean that plug, and I'll put it back in."

"Yes, Master. You didn't come again. Is that okay?"

"Yeah, I'm fine. After supper you can blow me for dessert."

Sawyer chuckled softly, nuzzling his jaw. "I would love to."

"I thought you might." He groaned as Sawyer pulled off. He didn't like separating at all.

"I'll bring you a warm cloth, Sir." Sawyer took the plug with him.

God. Was this real?

He sat back on the couch, watching as Sawyer washed the plug and soaked a cloth in water. It felt real and surreal at the same time. The thought had him smiling. Either way, he was holding on and not letting go.

CHAPTER ELEVEN

SAWYER WOKE up in Derek's arms, naked and hard, rubbing and wanting his lover, his new master?

Did he have a new master?

Did Derek want this?

Derek grumbled in his sleep and grabbed Sawyer's ass, fingers wrapping around one buttcheek and holding on.

Sawyer moaned softly, pushing back into the touch, testing Derek's intentions.

Derek's eyes blinked open, and he smiled. "Oh, Sawyer. Good morning." The hand on his ass didn't let go.

"Good morning. How are you?" He leaned forward and took a long, slow kiss.

"I don't know. Ask me after we've made love." Derek grinned, eyes twinkling.

Derek's hands began to wander as they kissed, seemingly randomly over his ass, the tops of his thighs and his back, but then Derek found the base of the plug, fingers touching it lightly, too lightly to be more than a tease, but there was a promise of so much more in the light touches.

He spread wide, humping down against his lover, his morning wood aching.

"You're so pretty in how you need." Derek rubbed their cheeks together, then pointed his tongue and traced Sawyer's lips.

He felt tingles wherever Derek's tongue touched, and the aching in his flesh increased.

Derek tapped the base of the plug again, harder this time. "We should go shopping online today. Get some plugs that belong to us."

"I'd love that. You can choose some to play with."

"They'll have to be pretty big. I know that's how you like them." Derek was clearly paying attention and remembering things Sawyer did and said. It was sweet and kind and something a master would do.

"Yes, Master. I'm a bit of an ass slut. I love to be full and needing." He whispered the words into Derek's ear.

Derek's erection jerked against his belly. "I know. I gotta admit, hearing you talk dirty is a real turn-on. Do you like that too? Do you like to hear about how I'm going to find a bunch of plugs, all different shapes, to fuck and fill you with?" Derek whispered too, making the conversation feel even more intimate.

"God yes." He had missed this, so much. "I can take it, take you and your will. I love the burn, the ache, the way you stare at my ass when it's plugged."

"I have to be honest, Sawyer—I stare at your ass, period." Derek gave him a cheeky grin. "But I can't look away when it's plugged. It makes you walk like… like you're moving just for me." Derek gave the base of the plug a few more taps as he talked about it.

"Yes, Master." He hummed softly. Derek liked to hear him talk, did he? "Have you read about fisting, Master? About milking?"

"Oh God." Derek drove against Sawyer's belly, dotting his skin with drops of precome. "Luke lent me a couple books, and I'm pretty sure there were sections about those…."

That was his cue to tell Derek about them, about how much he was into them.

"I would let you in, let you fill me with your hand. Can you imagine it, my ring snapping around your wrist as you took me?"

"Fuck yes. Well, no, I have no idea what that would feel like, but I want to know. We need to stock up on lube." Derek grabbed the base of the plug and began moving it out and back in again, fucking him with it.

"Yes. We need lube so you can stretch me, push me." He groaned softly and sucked on Derek's earlobe. "You can touch me everywhere, milk me dry. That's so wild, to need to come and come and have nothing left."

"Fuck. It sounds so much sexier when you say it." Derek pulled the plug right out, leaving him empty, but then pushed in a single finger, wriggling it around inside him. "Gonna re-lube you and then make love to you. Can't wait to get tested, to be able to feel your skin right against mine. I never have before. Never."

"I only did with my husband. You're my second lover."

"I find that super hot. I know I shouldn't, but I do."

"You'll be able to trap your seed inside me. No one else will touch me like you do." He groaned softly, imagining the wild need of having his gland stroked until he was sobbing and empty, his orgasms totally controlled.

"Fuck yes. You're mine, only mine, and nobody else will do that. No one." Derek grabbed the lube and slicked his fingers up. Then he plunged two of them into Sawyer's ass. "I'm going to make you fly, give you what you need."

"Yes!" He rolled his cock against Derek's belly and pulled one leg up.

"The milking thing." Derek pushed his fingertips against Sawyer's gland, making him jerk and moan. "It starts with this, right? Hitting your gland until you come, and then just keep hitting it?"

"Pet it. Nice and steady. Over and over until there's nothing left inside me." Oh sweet Jesus, he was going to die.

"I can do that. Will it still be good if I make love to you when you're empty? I couldn't tell from the stuff I read." Derek was so sweet. And he kept touching, fingertips so good and gentle against Sawyer's gland, building his pleasure up, his need to come getting stronger.

"It'll make me crazy. I'll need and need." He rolled up with a moan. "Imagine wanting to shoot, needing to, but there's nothing but electricity and hunger. I'll be begging you to touch me, fuck me, fill me up and help me."

"Oh God. I'm glad I called in last night and said I was taking today and tomorrow off so I could have a four-day weekend with you."

Derek's gentle touches kept on. It seemed he was a fast learner. He was already driving Sawyer crazy, and he was only just learning. He would be devastating with some experience under his belt.

His eyes rolled as precome began to slip from him, leaking and sliding down his shaft.

"Oh, it's working."

"Yes, Master. Please. Empty me." He could beg.

Derek moaned, clearly enjoying it when he did beg—Sawyer had never heard of a master who didn't.

"You're so tight and so hot inside. I love doing this, hearing how it affects you in your voice, feeling the results against my skin."

"You own my come, Master, my pleasure, my need. You choose how I shoot, if my balls are empty and all I can do is dry-come." He writhed, trying to get harder touches, but Derek refused to budge. Proving again that he was paying attention and that he was a quick learner.

"You'll come from this and just this until you can't come anymore. Then I'll make love to you."

Derek's words made him writhe harder.

Derek nuzzled his jaw. "So good. So good, pet."

"Pet?" He groaned, his toes curling.

"Uh-huh. Mine to keep and to pleasure and to be master of." Derek didn't ask if it was okay, and Sawyer was pretty sure that yesterday he probably would have. More signs of growing confidence in the role of master. If Derek kept this up, all of Sawyer's worries about whether or not Derek really wanted this were going to fade.

"Yes, Sir. Please. I ache."

"Good. You asked to."

He had, and it felt so good, so right. He felt... as close to complete as he had since before James had died. And he didn't want to be disloyal, but James was dead and he was alive, and it had been so long ago.

Derek pegged his gland a little harder, making him gasp. "Stay with me. I want you to know who is touching you."

"I know. I swear. I know." His hips and legs moved restlessly as that touch drove him mad.

"Show me, then. Come for me. Not just because of what I'm doing, but because I told you to. Me. Derek. Your master. Yours." Derek didn't work his gland any harder, but he did move faster, the touches absolutely undeniable. "This is orgasm one. How many are there in those sweet balls?"

Knowing him? Three for sure, maybe four or even five, although he'd be crazed by then.

"I said come, pet. Do it now." Derek did hit his gland a little harder this time, like an exclamation mark to his words.

He shot with a harsh moan, his eyes rolling back in his head. Derek pressed kisses over his face and, to his delight, didn't stop pegging his gland. The sweet, wonderful, crazy-making touches continued.

There was one difference, though; Derek worked a third finger in with the first two, stretching him wider. "Mmm... that's one."

Derek moved to kneel between his legs, eyes on his hole, watching him. It made him feel exposed, open, vulnerable.

He thought that might bother him a lot, with someone not James, but he trusted Derek. The guy had a good heart and had been nothing but eager and sweet and kind to him.

The touches never eased, steady and constant, his cock pouring cream. Derek began to lap at his skin, taking in the liquid his cock was depositing. It was incredible against his belly, but when Derek moved to clean his cock as well, tongue working the sides, then the head and his slit, the only thing that kept him from coming again was sheer willpower and experience as a sub.

He wanted this to be amazing for both of them. He wanted it to go on and on.

Derek worked his slit with the same diligence he showed with Sawyer's gland, the pointed tongue pressing into him. "Come for me again," Derek said after Sawyer had keened several times in a row.

"Master...."

"Now." Derek pushed his tongue deep into Sawyer's cockslit, making it sting, and it was all over. He shot again, his balls throbbing.

Derek caught it all in his mouth this time and lingered to suck on the head of his prick, pulling out more drops.

Sawyer knew he wasn't empty yet, but he didn't think he could possibly shoot again. Derek continued milking him, seeming convinced otherwise. Sawyer's head knew Derek was right, even if his body was trying to deny it.

"Not going to stop until you've given me every last drop that's inside you. Until you've given me everything."

"Master.... Master, please...." He needed it to stop, to go on and on forever.

"Love that," Derek admitted. "Becoming addicted to the sound of you calling me master." Derek moved to lick his balls, fingers still playing inside him, still insisting he give everything to Derek. "You still have spunk in here, pet. I know you do."

Derek was right, but it still made him whimper. He was a ball of sensation, every touch sparking a fire that was burning ever higher. He felt like he was going to pass out from pleasure, though he didn't. Instead, the pleasure simply continued to build, and even the smallest touch had a huge result now.

He could feel himself leaking, feel globs of need slide from the tip of his cock.

Derek dragged his tongue over Sawyer's balls again and again, then ran it slowly down the patch of skin beyond his balls, pressing firmly. He could feel it approaching his hole, but then Derek slid it back up to lick where his perineum and his balls met.

Derek nudged Sawyer's gland from both directions now, over and over. He was losing his fucking mind.

"You're allowed to come now, as much as you need to. As much as you can. Until you can't anymore." Derek's tongue flicked across his hole where it was stretched around Derek's invading fingers. Then Derek got his mouth around a part of his skin and began to suck.

He screamed with pleasure, his cock jerking with it, pulsing hard.

Derek continued to stimulate his hole, slowly working his way around the entire ring, licking and sucking and keeping him keyed up and needing. He drummed his feet against the mattress, trying not to just open his mouth and wail.

The strokes and nudges to his cock never stopped, never slowed, and he began to shake, his body overwhelmed.

"You still have more for me, don't you." Derek sounded so sure, his words less a question and more a statement of fact. "Come on. Let me have the rest so I can make love to you." Derek licked the new drops from his belly and sucked more out of his cockhead.

"Please. I can't...." He could trust Derek enough to be needy, for Derek to push him over the edge and follow through.

"You can, pet. You will. For me." Derek cleaned his cock again, then looked at it closely. "I'll know you're done when I can clean your slit and nothing new leaks out." Derek licked away the few drops that slid out of him at Derek's words. "See? You're still leaking. Still."

"You're making me. I'm yours."

"Making you is the point." Derek looked back down between his legs, at his hole, still touching his gland.

Everything took on a fuzzy hue, like his senses were compensating for the magnificent touches, putting all his attention on his cock and his hole.

"Look at how stretched you are, how pink and puffy. Your cock is still dripping. You do need this, don't you?"

Derek wasn't wrong. He hadn't been touched by anyone since James died, until Derek had given him that first blow job the day he'd moved in. And since then he'd felt full—good, but overloaded with spunk.

"Come on, pet, you're almost there, I can tell. And I want so badly to be inside you, to drive into you."

"Please. Please, I want your cock. I want you to fuck me."

"As soon as you're dry, pet."

He'd been testing, pushing, and Derek had passed with flying colors, keeping to his guns. It made him moan and buck, even more turned on, as impossible as that was.

Derek rubbed and rubbed, and he reached down, grabbed his nipples and pulled.

"Hey!" Derek stopped moving his fingers. "You aren't allowed to do that."

"No?"

"Pushing, pushing." Derek waited for him to let go, then started touching again. "You can always beg me to either touch them or let you do it yourself. But there's no touching unless I say so."

"Yes, Master." Utter pleasure flooded him and made him moan.

"Your cock is leaking again. You have to be almost empty at this point." Derek hit his gland hard a few times in a row, making his entire body jerk. "You like it when I remind you that your body isn't yours to touch—it's mine. What would be the best punishment, I wonder? I think you like spanking too much for that to be anything but fun."

He would let Derek discover that, ponder that, and make a decision about what would be the most effective.

"Something that cuts you off from touch, maybe…." Derek kissed him suddenly. "So far I haven't had to punish you. You're so different from Benny. I'm glad."

"I'm me. I try to be good. I try hard."

Derek nodded. "I can tell. And I like that. I like you. I try to be good too." Derek kissed him, fingers twisting and stretching inside him, then hitting his gland a few more times. "Are you empty yet, Sawyer? Do I need to tug on all your rings to make sure?"

"Please. Please, I need help."

"All you had to do was ask." Instead of using his free hand to tug Sawyer's nipple rings, Derek bent and took one into his mouth. Then he twisted as he pulled, yanking it good and hard, and Sawyer felt it all the way to his balls.

A huge drop of come oozed from his aching slit, his balls raw. Derek rolled his balls with that free hand, pushing them hard, squeezing them. He cried out and jerked, and his prick strained, another two watery pulses dribbling from him.

Derek's fingers slid out of him, and then his lover cleaned him up with a cloth. "I think that's about it, eh?" Derek pinched his cock, smiling as nothing came out. "My empty pet."

All Sawyer could do was moan.

Derek slicked his fingers up again, and then pushed the lube into his ass. It was cool, a little bit shocking after the heat from Derek's fingers, and he cried out, bucking. But not a drop slid from his cock.

"Oh, you're on fire."

"Will be for a day, at least."

"Lucky me." Derek didn't linger in his ass, pulling his fingers out quickly before grabbing a condom and working it on. Sawyer turned over, offering his ass eagerly, wagging his hips, trying to get attention.

"On your back, pet. I want to see your face while we make love." Derek kissed the base of his spine, then flipped him.

He grabbed his knees and tugged them back, spreading himself wide. Derek watched as he pushed his cock into Sawyer's hole. Once he was seated, Derek looked up, meeting Sawyer's eyes as he began to thrust.

Sawyer moaned softly, his body burning with use, thrumming happily. Derek found a pace, pushing into him over and over.

His prick was flagging, but the burn every time Derek slid past his gland was maddening and wonderful. Derek pushed harder, faster. Sawyer could read the pleasure in Derek's face and knew it probably wouldn't be long—his master so turned on already.

"Fuck me, Master. Make me yours."

"You are mine!" Derek slammed in harder, bringing their bodies together with force.

"Yes!" He wanted to come again, wanted to touch himself, wanted to scream.

Finding his gland, Derek stayed right there, gaze holding his. Then Derek grabbed his cock, squeezing him tight as the fucking continued.

"Oh, fuck. Fuck. You… I can't…."

"Can't what?" Derek asked. "Long as it feels good, that's all that matters."

"Yes. So good. It's so good. The ache, the stretch." He was babbling and he knew it.

"Uh-huh." Derek nodded, pushing in even harder. His body was limned with sweat, his muscles working. He was gorgeous, moving above Sawyer.

Sawyer met each and every thrust, driving up toward Derek to give him pleasure. Derek groaned.

"Don't want it to end."

"No… it never has to end."

"Can't fuck you forever," Derek noted. "But I can keep coming back to it."

"Yes, Master." He'd meant more globally, but he understood.

Derek leaned in, kissing him. The change of position brought Derek's cock up to his gland and pounded against it.

He gasped, scrabbling at Derek's shoulders, cries winging from him. That was clearly Derek's cue to stay right there and hit his gland like his cock was a hammer.

His entire body convulsed, electricity slamming through him, clawing up his spine.

"Yes!" Derek cried out in triumph and froze, face going lax.

He kept jerking restlessly, whimpering and exhausted. Derek collapsed down onto him, lips warm against his skin, the big hands sliding over his body, soothing him.

"Easy, pet. Breathe. You did so well." Derek began to stroke his cock, sweet and slow. Derek was going to make him lose his mind.

The thrusting and sweet touches continued, Derek looking like he was going to keep pushing until Sawyer fainted from the pleasure.

God, he was a lucky man. Totally lucky and taken.

CHAPTER TWELVE

BENNY BEBOPPED up the stairs to the front door, the smell of something good pouring from Sawyer's apartment. Pot roast. Uhn.

Luke popped his head out of Sawyer's apartment. "Hey, babe. We're eating down here tonight."

"Yeah? It smells good." He went to Luke, reaching for that outstretched hand.

Luke took his hand and tugged him in for a kiss. "Welcome home, baby. Smile—it's the weekend."

"It is. Hey, lover." He melted against Luke, catching a glimpse of Sawyer, naked and plugged and in Derek's lap, writhing. "Whoa."

Luke followed his gaze and chuckled. "Yeah, the kid is learning to be a Dom by leaps and bounds. I think he's going to keep Sawyer very busy."

"Was he naughty?" He sort of liked that idea, Sawyer being punished.

"You think he's being punished?" Luke asked. "Trust me—he's not being punished." Luke ushered him in, locking the door.

"Bummer." He winked.

Laughing, Luke took his hand and brought him into the living room. Luke sat. "Okay, Benny. Strip for me."

"What? Before supper?"

"It's in the slow cooker. We can eat whenever."

Benny frowned at Luke and glanced over at Sawyer and Derek, who were wrapped up in each other. Derek whispered into Sawyer's ear, and Sawyer went wild.

"What's up, Luke?" He stayed in Luke's arms, stayed close.

"We haven't all played together since last weekend. And we haven't really honestly played together." Luke brought him in for another kiss. He opened up, moaning softly into his lover's mouth. He was in a good mood, was ready for the weekend, was ready to play.

As they were kissing, Sawyer cried out, the sound full pleasure. Luke smiled and nuzzled him. "Sounds like they're done."

"What's up with them?" he asked again.

Luke looked at him, one eyebrow raised. "They're hot for each other."

"Ah, I remember that," he teased.

Luke chuckled. "Benny's here, boys."

Derek and Sawyer both looked over at him, Sawyer rather glassy-eyed.

"Hey." Derek gave him a grin.

"Hello, Benny." Sawyer looked utterly fucked.

"You guys finished for now?" Luke asked.

"My master didn't get to come yet," Sawyer noted.

Derek chuckled. "I was thinking I could get a blow job, actually."

"Yes, Master." Sawyer slid down between his thighs.

Derek groaned, spreading his legs wide, and Sawyer undid his top button.

Luke nodded at Derek. "You think Sawyer's the only one who should get a reward like that?"

"No. I think Benny should suck me too."

"Hey! You're not my boss!"

"Benny." Luke slapped the side of his ass. "No one said he was your boss, but I am your master, and I too think you should work his cock next to Sawyer." Luke whispered into his ear, "You'll look so hot."

He pouted a little bit. "What about you?"

"Oh, the two of you can take care of me after you're finished with Derek. As long as he gives you a good grade." Luke's smile was evil.

The temptation to pinch Luke was huge. Huge. He didn't do it, because he was still in a good mood, but the temptation was there.

"Come on, boy. Help Sawyer suck me." Derek sounded like he wasn't all there, Sawyer licking at his cock like it was a Popsicle.

"Not your boy. You and me, we're friends." Luke was his Dom, dammit.

"Then come suck my cock already, Benny—you're usually not shy." Derek grinned at him. "Please, dude. I want to see you and Sawyer together. You're so fucking pretty together."

That was all he needed, that affection, that *please*. "Okay, man. Your prick is sweet as fuck."

He moved to kneel beside Sawyer, clothed where Sawyer was naked.

Derek groaned, hands moving to slide through his and Sawyer's hair. Sawyer stopped long enough to give him a little smile, but the guy still looked half-drugged from sex.

"You look well fucked." He stole a quick kiss from Sawyer, whose lips were swollen and hot.

Their lips parted, and Sawyer gave him a blissed-out smile. "Uh-huh." Then Sawyer turned back to Derek's impressive cock and licked it from bottom to top.

"Lucky guy." He took the other side, going the other direction.

"We had the day off," murmured Derek, the words ending on a groan.

"Lucky guys," Luke said.

"We've got the weekend to play, the four of us." Derek reached down to pinch Sawyer's nipple. "I milked him, Benny. I milked him hard, and he's so needy."

Benny's eyes rolled back in his head. Oh fuck.

"Can you imagine that, babe?" Luke asked him. "What that would feel like?"

"It's so good. I need so much, and I can't," Sawyer said.

He reached for Sawyer's cock. "No?"

"No."

"And that's good?" Benny asked. He wasn't entirely sure.

"God, yes." Sawyer grinned. "Yes."

Sawyer was half-hard, but he cried out in need as soon as Benny touched, beginning to fuck his hand.

"You don't have my permission to do that," growled Derek.

They both looked up at Derek, and his cock went hard in his jeans. Fuck.

"No, Master. I'm sorry, Master." Sawyer bent his head.

"I won't punish you. This time. But don't do it again without my permission. Either of you."

"I won't make you get in trouble," Benny promised Sawyer. "Don't worry. I'm not mean."

Sawyer kissed him again, gently. "Thank you."

"Stay on task, boys," Luke told them.

"Yeah, my cock isn't going to suck itself."

Benny looked up, finding Derek trying hard not to laugh. He rolled his eyes playfully. "That was bad."

Sawyer leaned down and began to wrap his lips around the shaft of Derek's cock. He went for the tip, slapping the slit with his tongue.

"Fuck!" Oh yeah, Derek wasn't laughing now.

He heard Sawyer hum, the sound pleased, satisfied. Sawyer headed south toward Derek's balls, so he focused on the tip, on making Derek scream. He was good at this; he knew how to make it happen.

"God, the two of you are stunning," Derek told them.

"Amen," added Luke. "I love the plug sticking from Sawyer's ass. It makes him push his ass out."

"My pet has a stunning ass, doesn't he?"

"It's lovely. Soft and round. My boy's ass begs to be pink and heated."

Benny shook his head. He didn't like the spankings. Sawyer, on the other hand, was busy moaning like a huge spanking slut.

"What? You don't like it when I ask you to spread yourself and ask me to whip your hole, boy?"

He shook his head around Derek's cockhead.

"Liar," murmured Luke, whose voice was husky enough he knew the sight of the three of them was turning him on.

He pulled harder, moaning low, and Derek arched, pushing into his lips. "God...."

He could hear Sawyer licking and lapping at Derek's balls, the noises sexy as hell, and Benny was turned on more than he wanted to be. It was hot, though, doing this with Sawyer, making Derek need hard.

"Kiss Benny, pet. Kiss him over the tip of my cock."

"Yes, Master." Sawyer licked his way back up, kissing Benny with barely hidden desperation.

Benny couldn't help but kiss back, tongue sliding across Derek's cock to get to Sawyer's mouth.

Sawyer moaned into his lips, and he could see how Sawyer was thrusting, working the plug inside him.

Derek had him fucking wild and needy. It was impressive.

Benny couldn't decide if he was jealous or grateful it wasn't him. Or whether he wanted Derek giving Luke ideas or not. Who'd have thought the kid had it in him?

"Pay attention, Benny." Derek's voice had that growl in it again, and it sent shivers down his spine.

He slapped the tip of Derek's cock, hard. Derek grunted, hips bucking and sending his cock deep into Benny's mouth.

Benny pulled hard, then popped off, letting Sawyer take over for a few desperate sucks. They shared Derek back and forth like that, Derek moaning constantly.

"That's it," growled Luke. "You've got him now."

He backed off as the heavy cock swelled, letting Sawyer have Derek's spunk. Sawyer's lips parted around Derek, and he moaned loudly, then began to swallow.

Benny found himself swallowing. He knew what that tasted like, how Derek's spunk felt on his tongue. Still, Sawyer was bucking, fucking himself on the plug.

He looked to Luke.

Before Luke could say anything, Derek's voice sounded. "Stop that, pet. Don't make me punish you."

"Master...."

"Over my knees, Sawyer. Now."

Was this Derek?

Benny moved to Luke as Sawyer draped himself over Derek's lap. Derek began to tap the base of the plug, over and over, making Sawyer sob and writhe. The man's prick was between Derek's legs, sliding with every movement. Sawyer was wild. Absolutely wild.

"Look at him, boy. He's out of his mind. The controlled sub, completely gone." Luke tugged Benny's shirt out of his jeans.

"How is this Derek?" He whispered because he didn't want to insult Derek, but it just... he'd never seen this strength, this... mastery before. Not from Derek.

"He's found his sub, and it has woken that strength up inside him. They've been at it for two days, learning how to work together."

"Weird. Hot, but weird." Benny lifted his arms up so Luke could pull his shirt off.

"You telling me it doesn't make you hot?" Luke asked, putting a hand in his lap.

"No. Look at that."

Sawyer begged Derek, hair dark with sweat as Derek worked his ass. Sawyer was mostly hard, fucking Derek's thighs. "Master, I need."

"I know." The plug was tugged out, slammed in. "You disobeyed, pet."

Benny moaned. Fuck. Fucking shit. They looked incredible together.

Luke slid his fingers along Benny's waistband, teasing. "Are you hard, boy?"

"God, yes."

"Me too. I've been hard since I got home and first saw them." Popping his top button, Luke slid his hand in, cupping Benny's erection.

"Master." He leaned harder, tilting his head for a kiss, even as he watched Derek punish Sawyer.

Luke devoured his mouth, tongue pushing in and tasting him. The hand around his cock tightened, Luke beginning to stroke. Oh, that was good. That was what he needed. Just that.

Luke pulled out of the kiss long enough to give him a single order. "No coming until I say so, boy."

"I won't. I'm good for you." Mostly. Sometimes.

"Except when you don't want to be," Luke noted, giving him a knowing smile.

"Or when I need not to be." Know thyself. He loved playing with Luke, loved being the brat, but sometimes he just needed and needed hard.

Luke's expression softened, and he cupped Benny's cheek. "I love you, Benny. You know that, eh?"

"I do. I know." He leaned forward for a kiss.

Luke gave it to him, opening his mouth, tongue sliding right in. Yeah. He knew. It was more than simply the sex that told him. Luke wasn't just some hot guy he got off with. Hell, neither was Derek.

It occurred to him suddenly that maybe Derek wouldn't need them anymore. At the same time, he wasn't going to take orders from Derek. He just wasn't. He wasn't ever going to be a sub like Sawyer was either, so if Luke was getting ideas from watching Sawyer....

Luke bit his lower lip, hard, like he'd known Benny was busy thinking when he should have been paying attention to Luke's kisses. The sharp nip made him jerk, and he growled a little, pushing into the hand that still toyed with his cock. Luke eased his hand out of Benny's jeans in response, making him groan in protest.

"We should try the milking." Luke toyed with his zipper, pulling it down tooth by tooth at a snail's pace.

What? No. Benny shook his head. That looked like torture—Sawyer was totally out of control.

"Easy," Luke murmured, fingers sliding along his belly, his very tight belly. All his muscles were stiff, hard, but he began relaxing as Luke nuzzled his neck and petted him. "I was only teasing. I know what you need, and as hot as the milking is on Sawyer, it's not in our wheelhouse. Maybe one day we'll push your limits in that direction, but for now, we're good."

"It's not my thing." He was pretty damn sure about that.

Luke chuckled and rubbed their cheeks together. "Like I said, I know what you need."

His zipper was finally down, and Luke patted his package for a moment, still not working his hand back in to grab it.

"Stand for me and let's get these jeans off."

That he could get behind. Or in front of. Whatever. Benny stood and pushed his jeans off, his underwear going with them. The material all pooled at his ankles, and he stepped out of them by moving to stand between Luke's legs. His prick was hard and eager and right at Luke's eye level. He couldn't deny how turned on he was from watching Derek and Sawyer together.

When Luke ran his tongue around the head of Benny's cock, he didn't care what had turned him on—this was what was going to make him come.

Luke wrapped his lips around Benny's cockhead and worked his slit with a pointed tongue. The stretch stung in the best way, and his balls began to ache.

"Gonna make me come, Luke," he warned.

Luke shook his head, the movement adding a special something to the suction. Then Luke pulled off. "Not until I say so, boy."

Benny swallowed his protest and nodded instead. "I told you I was good for you. I won't." He just hoped he could keep to that. Especially when Luke tightened his lips and increased the suction. Benny grabbed Luke's head without thinking, moaning loudly.

Luke's smile felt weird around his prick, and Benny would lay odds on it being a wicked smile. Especially when warm fingers grasped his balls, Luke stroking them, rolling them in their sac.

Whimpering, Benny spread his legs, giving Luke more access. Luke took advantage immediately, stroking the skin beyond his balls with a barely-there touch. That made the sudden hard pressure against his gland from the outside surprising, and he bucked without even meaning to, his cock pushing deep into Luke's throat. He tightened his fingers in Luke's hair, crying out as he nearly came.

Oh fuck, that had been close.

"Master." He moaned the word out as Luke pressed that spot again. "I'm not going to be able to hold it back. Not if you do that."

Luke's fingers gentled again, the strokes maddeningly soft now.

He took a few panting breaths, trying to recapture his equilibrium. Each of Sawyer's cries sent shivers along his spine, though, the ecstatic sounds alone keeping him on edge. When combined with Luke's mouth on his cock and that constant barely-there touch along his perineum, he was almost as close as he had been moments ago.

"Please. Please, Master, I need." Benny wasn't above begging.

"What do you need, boy?" Fuck, Luke could be a tease when he wanted to.

"You. To come. Anything you'll give me. Everything." A shudder went through him as Luke pressed a finger against his hole without actually pushing in. He cried out, bucking again, but Luke was ready for it this time and moved his head so Benny didn't push any deeper into Luke's mouth.

Luke held him right there, finger at his ass, tongue touching his slit, but didn't otherwise move or suck. It was like they'd frozen in this position. Benny wailed softly.

"Whatever you choose to give me. Please, Master, that's what I want."

He could almost hear the "Good, boy," though Luke couldn't have said it, because his mouth was still around Benny's cock. Luke took him in to the root, and Benny tightened his fingers in Luke's hair to keep from holding Luke in place and fucking his mouth. That would earn him a spanking at best.

His patience was rewarded, Luke bobbing his head, pulling almost all the way off Benny's cock before taking it all back in and swallowing around the tip. Benny sobbed as it continued. Luke was so good to him, loving on him like nobody else ever had, ever could.

He wailed when Luke pulled off, but the words "You can come now" preceded the sudden resumption of Luke's blow job. It only took two more swallows and a threat of teeth dragging over his cock before Benny came, his cry ringing through the room as Luke took his pleasure in. The orgasm seemed to go on and on as Luke kept sucking, and when his master's mouth finally pulled off him, Benny's knees went out from under him.

Luke caught him, pulling him into his master's lap.

He curled into Luke's chest, panting. When he'd finally caught his breath, he realized that Sawyer and Derek were quiet now, and he glanced over to find Derek watching him and Luke, Sawyer fast asleep in his arms.

It made him blush somehow, which was crazy. Derek had seen him and Luke lots of times, often just watching, especially if he'd had his orgasm first. Then Derek smiled at him, and it wasn't some aloof or knowing "master" smile, it was Derek's easygoing, happy grin, and Benny smiled back at him.

Okay, so not everything had changed. And he was sure that any minute now Luke was going to demand a blow job of his own or something, which he was very much looking forward to giving, but right this second, he was going to revel in the sensation of feeling melted and sated and let Luke hold him close.

Chapter Thirteen

LUKE WOKE up a little before six as usual. He knew that sleeping in for just a couple of days tended to mess with his schedule, and while he would on occasion, he tended not to. He liked having a schedule. He tugged his arm from beneath Benny and rolled to his back, stretching. Benny snuffled and pushed closer to the body on the other side of him. A glance proved that was Sawyer, who gave a small sigh and cuddled right in with Benny. It looked like Derek was already up. And that was surprising.

He slipped out of bed and grabbed one of the robes on the back of Sawyer's door. Wait. There were three robes there. He had to presume that Derek was already wearing one. Sawyer had picked up robes for each of them. Benny was right—the man was the sweetest and the subbyest. He was glad they were here for Sawyer. The guy would have been lost if he'd landed somewhere he had to hide his true nature. He guessed that had been the plan—ignore his own needs. It was lucky for all of them Sawyer had rented here.

The emerald robe was silky and cool—perfect for the current weather. It made him wonder if warmer ones would appear for the winter. It wouldn't surprise him if they did.

He found Derek—wearing the same robe in a ruby red—in the kitchen, pulling a steaming mug out of the microwave. Derek offered him an easygoing smile.

"Hey, Luke. You want some hot cocoa? Sawyer made it yesterday so we could warm it up as we wanted it." Derek grabbed a bag of mini marshmallows and put a bunch into his mug.

"That sounds great." Luke grabbed himself a mug, noting that the coffee maker was full and ready to go with a push of the On button, while the electric kettle sat on its element, already full of water, a little tea caddy with several kinds of tea right next to it. Sawyer's man had trained him incredibly well.

Derek grabbed a pitcher from the fridge, popped the lid, and poured the cold cocoa into his mug.

Luke set the mug into the microwave. "How long?"

"I did mine for two minutes on level eight, and it's only barely too hot." Derek lounged against the counter and buried his nose in his mug, breathing deeply.

Getting the microwave running, Luke warmed his cocoa. He wasn't much of a coffee drinker—it wasn't great for the body. "You're up early."

Derek shrugged. "I guess so. I woke up wide-awake, if you know what I mean, and instead of tossing and risking waking everyone up, I figured I'd get out of bed."

"You got stuff on your mind?" Luke asked.

Derek shrugged again. This time the move was even more casual—but less authentic. "I guess."

"You wanna talk?" The microwave beeped, and Luke pulled his cocoa out. It was steaming lightly, so obviously hot enough, as Derek had predicted. He added three of the little marshmallows to it.

"Let's go sit in the living room," Derek suggested. "The kitchen chairs are pretty hard."

"Imagine sitting on them wearing a plug." Luke guessed that was the reason there were no cushions on the chairs. They were meant to give a man wearing a plug quite the workout. He could picture Sawyer sitting and squirming. He could picture Benny right next to him, doing exactly the same thing but being far more vocal about how unfair it all was.

He followed Derek into the living room, grunting approvingly when Derek chose to sit on the couch. Conversations about intimate things deserved to be had in close quarters. He sat as well, the two of them not quite touching, but close enough that he could feel Derek's body heat.

Derek took a careful sip of his cocoa and sat back with a happy sigh. "Perfect."

"Sawyer enjoys doing things for his lovers."

"Yeah. He's amazing. I felt bad that he was making all our meals, but he keeps insisting that it makes him feel good to do that kind of thing. To serve." The words were spoken like Derek was testing them out.

"That's exactly how he sees it—that he's serving us. You. Service is a very important part of BDSM for some subs." Hell, there were as many *types* of subs as there were subs. They could be hugely different in temperament and needs, like Sawyer and Benny, though the two of them also had much in common.

"I guess I worry that he's doing everything for me and I'm not doing anything for him."

Luke snorted at that. "Come on, Dee—I saw him yesterday. He was blissed-out. Like absolutely. And now he's in the bedroom, sleeping deep and hard. I bet he hasn't slept as well as this since his husband got sick. He needs what you're giving him."

"Yeah, I'm beginning to see that." Derek took a bigger sip of his cocoa. It had obviously cooled down enough because he took a second sip, this one a whole mouthful.

Luke went ahead and tested his own, pleased that it was cool enough too. "Damn, this is good. We're all going to benefit from Sawyer's need to serve. I suggested to him that we could all contribute to the pot for groceries and his contribution could be to cook for us. I didn't mean to step on any toes—you hadn't laid your claim yet."

Derek's cheeks pinked, and he ducked his head. "It sounds so… possessive when you say it like that."

"Do you feel possessive about him?"

"Well, yeah."

"Then it's an appropriate way to put it. I knew you had it in you, but I have to admit, you've taken to it like a fish to water. You've progressed a lot faster than I would have expected."

"I want to be what he needs me to be. No, I need to be what he needs me to be. I have no problem with the four of us being together, but it would make me crazy if he had to turn to you for everything." Derek looked him in the eye. "I need to be the one to give it to him."

"I understand that," he told Derek gently. He really did. He'd been living it ever since he'd come out, after all. "Are you getting what you need from the relationship too?"

Derek laughed, cheeks going a darker red. "Oh yeah."

"I'm glad it's working out."

"Me too."

"You know if you have any questions or need anything, you can always come to me." He was totally there for Derek, and for Sawyer too.

"I know."

"How did you land on the milking?" He was curious. Out of everything in the books he'd given Derek, it was on the more extreme side of the scale.

"Sawyer told me about it. About how much he liked it."

That actually surprised Luke. "Oh?"

"Yeah. We were, uh...." Derek cleared his throat. "We were talking dirty to each other, and it came up."

"I bet that wasn't all that came up," he teased.

Derek laughed, and that seemed to relax him. "Things were kind of already up. Anyway, he asked if I'd read about fisting or milking, and of course I had, so... well, one thing led to another, and when it made him as wild as it did, it made me want to keep making him that way, to give him what he needs even more than I already did."

"You've already learned the most important lesson for being a Dom."

"I have?" Derek looked surprised.

"You're listening to your sub."

"Isn't that true for being anyone's lover?" Derek asked.

"It should be, Dee, it really should be. But it goes double for being a Dom."

Derek took another mouthful of his cocoa and was quiet for a few minutes. Luke could almost see the wheels turning in his head.

"So what's the second most important lesson?"

"The safeword."

"You mean that's really a thing. Like for everyone?"

Luke realized that Benny had never safeworded in front of Derek. Okay, so Benny had never safeworded period, but it wasn't something they'd discussed in front of Derek either. "The safeword is so that you can push your sub and he can deny that he wants what you're doing all he wants, but if he doesn't safeword, you know it's not more than he can take."

"But why would I want to do something to Sawyer that I know he doesn't want? Why wouldn't I listen when he says no or stop?"

"Well... for a lot of couples, pushing boundaries is an important aspect of BDSM. And if you're doing something that causes pain—pain that your sub wants—you might not notice when you push too far, you might not even realize that you have. So it's important to have a word that stops everything."

"I don't want to whip Sawyer. I don't want to make him hurt." Derek sounded very sure about that.

"What if he wants that from you?"

Derek sighed and stared down at his cup. He was quiet for long enough that Luke thought he wasn't going to answer the question. Then he sighed again. "I don't know if I could do it. But if I tell him that, he's going to say that's fine, he can live without it. But what if he really does need it?"

"You do have the advantage of a second Dom here," Luke noted.

"No." Derek's answer was immediate and firm. "If he needs it, I'll figure it out, come to you to learn how to do it. But I don't want you doing anything to him that I won't. I... I want to keep playing with you and Benny, but he's mine. I'm sorry?"

"You don't have to apologize for how you feel, Dee." In fact, Luke was pleased to hear the sentiments from Derek. It meant he was serious, that he was in it not only to make Sawyer happy, but because he felt that Sawyer was his. "And you know, you can bring up the safeword, bring up the whipping and whatnot, as one of the things you've read about and gauge how Sawyer feels based on that. In other words, find out if it's something he's into before you let him know how you feel. That way you'll get his honest answer."

"Oh, that's a really good idea."

He smirked. "I know. I've got a lot of them."

Derek rolled his eyes, but he was laughing too.

Luke waited for the laughter to die down. "Even if you aren't going to do any pain play at all, you do need that safeword."

"Okay, that's cool. Benny must have one, huh?"

"Yep. Broccoli."

"But he hates broccoli."

"He does—which means he'd only say it during sex if it's because he's safewording."

"Ah. That makes sense."

"Once you guys have a safeword, you need to share it with us. If we're all going to really play together, it's important we know it, like you needed to know Benny's now that you're becoming a Dom."

"How come you guys never told me before?" Derek asked.

Luke shrugged. "We never played hard enough when it was the three of us. And you were more sub than Dom, and like I said, we never pushed anything too hard when we were all together."

"Huh." Derek was quiet again.

"You've got a question about that?"

"I guess I never realized how serious the two of you were."

"We weren't when the three of us first got together, no. But over time Benny and I came to an understanding. And I love him. I mean, I love you too, don't get me wrong, but Benny is, well, you said it best about Sawyer—Benny is mine."

Derek nodded slowly. "I do get that. And I wouldn't have before."

"Would it have freaked you out if we'd told you about it?" Luke asked.

"Uh, yeah, probably." Derek finished his cocoa and put his cup aside. "This is pretty serious talk for six in the morning."

And that was Luke's cue that Derek had taken in about as much as he was ready to at this point. He could roll with that.

"It is. Especially when we've both got morning wood going on." His had gone down some, but Derek was still pretty young, and Luke could see that his hard-on was still waiting to be dealt with.

He put his own cup down before leaning in to bring their mouths together. Derek kissed him back eagerly, their breath mingling, the sweet taste of chocolate even nicer on Derek than it had been in his cup.

"Oh...." The word was more sigh than real sound, but both he and Derek heard it, and both of them looked up to see Sawyer trying to slip back into the bedroom unnoticed.

"Sawyer. Don't run away." Derek held out a hand. "We were just wrapping up a conversation."

"Is that what we're calling it now?" Sawyer's robe was golden, but otherwise just like his and Derek's. He moved unerringly toward Derek and took his hand.

Derek pulled Sawyer down onto his lap. "Well, we'd just moved from the actual talking portion of the conversation. And good morning."

Sawyer snuggled in and raised his head for a kiss. "Good morning."

Derek closed the distance between their lips, and the kiss lasted a good long time, making Luke's erection come back full force. When their lips parted, Derek whispered into Sawyer's ear, and Sawyer smiled, then turned to Luke, asking for a kiss from Luke. He gave it happily, enjoying the way Sawyer not only tasted different from Derek or Benny, but kissed differently as well. He would be able to tell which of his lovers was kissing him in the dark simply by how they kissed.

He cupped Sawyer's cheek and tilted his head slightly, then concentrated on the right side of Sawyer's mouth. Would Derek pick up on the invitation to join the kiss? Derek did indeed, pressing his lips against Luke's and Sawyer's both. Then he pushed his tongue in to be included there too. Luke groaned, enjoying the three-way.

He'd never shared a four-way kiss and wondered if it was possible. If it would feel as good as this did, or would it feel awkward and a lot of work to make sure everyone was getting something out of it.

As if thinking about him had conjured him up, Benny groaned behind them, and Luke glanced toward the sound in time to watch Benny head quickly for them, utterly naked. Then Benny pushed into the kiss, and it was awkward at first, but Luke didn't feel like anyone was left out. After some slips and bumps of lips against lips and quiet laughter, they suddenly clicked, and while it wasn't as deep as the three-way could go, it felt amazing to be kissing all his lovers at the same time.

"You guys started without me," Benny accused once the unique kiss had ended.

Sawyer reached up and touched Benny's cheek. "We were just saying good morning. I didn't want to wake you when I got up. You work so hard during the week."

Benny looked completely mollified by Sawyer's words. "Thanks, man. I appreciate it." He took a kiss of his own too, his and Sawyer's lips sliding together.

"There's a robe for you on the back of the bedroom door," Sawyer told Benny. "I hope you like the color."

Benny strode across the room and came back a moment later wearing the blue robe. "This rocks, though I'm not sure I can sit on Luke's lap with it—I'll slide right off."

"I can get something else if you don't like the silk," Sawyer offered right away.

"Nah. I'm just fooling." Benny sat firmly in between him and Derek, and Luke shifted to make room. "I'm not much of a lap-sitter anyway."

Luke didn't say anything, but he did give Benny a look. They had some of their best sex with Benny in his lap. Benny had the good grace to blush, and Luke let it go at that.

"Is everyone hungry for breakfast?" Sawyer asked. "I was thinking about breakfast muffins."

"Is that like bran muffins?" Benny asked. The man had an aversion to anything that even hinted at being healthy.

Sawyer shook his head. "Not at all. It's basically an egg with some cheese cooked in a bacon-lined muffin tin."

"Oh God, yes, please." Benny was practically drooling.

"That sounds delicious. I'm in." Luke was going to have to add more workout time into his schedule if they all agreed to have Sawyer be their full-time cook.

"Do you need any help?" Derek asked as Sawyer stood.

"Nope. It won't take me five minutes to get them in the oven, and by then the coffee should be ready too. I can't believe none of you turned the pot on!"

"We had the cocoa, which was delicious." Derek grinned and stood. "I'll turn it on now and help you get everyone a mug."

"As you wish." Sawyer leaned up and kissed the corner of Derek's mouth, and the two of them went to the kitchen, Derek's arm wrapped around Sawyer's waist.

Benny watched, then turned back to Luke. "I can't believe I have to wait five minutes for coffee, let alone however long it's going to be before we get actual food."

Luke leaned back and spread his legs. "Suck me, Benny."

"I thought you'd never ask!" Benny went to his knees and pushed the silk aside, pouncing as soon as Luke's cock pushed between the edges of the robe.

He didn't bother to point out that he hadn't asked and hadn't requested—he'd ordered. He was in the mood for a blow job, not a philosophical discussion about whether or not something was an order when it was exactly what the sub wanted. There'd be time enough for that, and right now he wanted to see if his eager Benny would be able to make him come before Derek and Sawyer were finished in the kitchen. As Benny's tongue swirled around the head of his cock, Luke was betting Benny totally could.

CHAPTER FOURTEEN

DEREK DIDN'T get a chance to talk to Sawyer about safewords and pain play until the following Wednesday. All four of them had spent the entire weekend together, and Derek was still a little shy about the whole being Sawyer's Dom thing in front of Luke and Benny. Maybe shy wasn't the right word, but it was new, and he hadn't wanted to have the discussion in front of Luke. He didn't want Luke to think he was doing the Dom thing wrong.

Monday night Sawyer had fallen asleep in his arms in front of the television right after supper, and on Tuesday Benny and Luke had stayed late after eating. They talked about it as a group and agreed to all contribute to the groceries, which Sawyer would then cook, providing them all with supper during the week and all meals during the weekend. Derek didn't get how doing all that cooking for everyone could be fun, but he couldn't deny how at peace Sawyer was while doing it.

Wednesday Luke had a late client, and Benny had decided to go do a workout so he could spend the time with Luke. With his newfound knowledge of exactly how serious Luke and Benny were about the whole Dom-and-sub thing, he had a hunch that Benny wanted the excuse to be ordered around by Luke in public. Nobody would think it anything kinky if Luke was shouting orders to Benny during a workout session. Unless Benny sprung persistent wood.

The thought made him grin.

"What's up?" Sawyer asked, coming to give him a kiss as he sat at the kitchen table watching Sawyer cook up something that smelled amazing.

"I was just thinking about Benny getting a hard-on during his workout with Luke."

"Do you think that would be embarrassing for him?" Sawyer asked, going back to stirring the contents of a large saucepan.

Derek thought about it, then shook his head. "No. I don't think he cares if other people can tell he's turned on."

"Maybe he gets a thrill from it," Sawyer suggested, like someone who knew from experience.

Huh. Derek wasn't sure he would want to do anything in front of anyone but Luke and Benny. A small voice at the back of his head made him admit to himself that he liked knowing Luke and Benny were watching. It did add a certain zing to things.

"Do you?" he asked.

"It depends on the situation. Under normal circumstances, not at all. I don't want to be hard in front of people in general. But at a club would be a different story."

"I'm not sure I could get into it in front of more than Luke and Benny." He had decided that he wasn't going to worry if he and Sawyer liked different things. There was clearly lots of stuff they both liked doing, and if they came up with stuff that one of them wanted and the other didn't, they could talk about it, compromise. Maybe indulge in rarely.

"I liked it more for my master making me do it than it being a natural turn-on," Sawyer admitted. "And it only worked because he was so sure it was what he wanted us to be doing." Sawyer turned the heat down and covered his dish, then came back over to him. "There is nothing I can't live without, I promise. If all you want to do is kiss and do it missionary style, then that's what we'll do."

"That would probably get boring."

"I don't know—I could do nothing but kiss you forever." Sawyer spoke the words against his lips.

"You might have a point." He stopped talking in favor of kissing Sawyer. And kissing him, and kissing him. Until his ass started reminding him that Sawyer's kitchen chairs were hard.

"You want to move to the sofa?" Sawyer asked. It was amazing how Sawyer always seemed so in tune with him. Always catering to his needs. Even more amazing was how much Sawyer got out of that. Derek thought it was pretty damn special, being able to get such satisfaction of out serving others.

"What about your supper?" Sawyer had been working hard to make that.

"It'll keep warm until we're ready to eat it."

"It smells delicious."

"Mushroom and white wine risotto."

"Yum!" Derek loved how eating had become an adventure—it was like having access to a restaurant.

"We could eat now, but I haven't seen you all day and would love to spend some time with you first," Sawyer admitted.

"Like getting ourselves back into our together headspace after work," Derek suggested.

Sawyer beamed at him, face all lit up. "Exactly like that!"

Derek downed the bottle of soda Sawyer'd given him and headed for the living room. He sat in the recliner, pleased as punch when Sawyer plopped down in his lap. Sawyer curled in, and Derek wrapped his arms around him.

"So we've talked about how our days went and a little bit about how we feel about doing sexy things in public. Why don't you tell me some of the other stuff you like. I know from my research that there's lots of things we haven't talked about at all yet."

"Did I tell you how much I appreciate that you've been doing research?" Sawyer smiled at him, eyes sparkling. "I was worried you were doing it just to make me happy, but I can't believe you'd be as enthusiastic and willing as you are if it wasn't something you wanted too."

Derek nodded. "I didn't know that it was—but it is."

"And you'll tell me if you don't like something—like with the voyeurism."

"I will," Derek promised. "As long as you tell me about thing things you like and don't like too." He wasn't worried—Sawyer had been good about telling him so far. "On that topic—you should probably have a safeword."

Sawyer beamed at him. "You *have* been reading."

"Well, yeah. I said I had."

"But really reading in depth and paying attention." Sawyer kissed the side of his mouth. "You're a very special man, Derek."

"Well, so are you, so I guess we're a good match."

Sawyer chuckled. "Uh-huh."

"So what is?" Derek asked.

"What's what? Oh! My safeword."

"Yeah."

Sawyer chuckled again. "It's buffoon."

"That's different." Derek didn't think it was bad or anything, but it wasn't what he'd expected. Although now that he was thinking about it, he wasn't sure what kind of word he thought Sawyer might have.

"It's not a word I'd ever use, so it works well as a safeword."

"It does. Can I ask a question, and if you don't want to answer, that's okay. I know it's pretty personal and intimate."

"Go ahead." Sawyer met his gaze.

"Did you ever use your safeword with your husband?"

Sawyer nodded. "Once. I was scared about what he was asking me to do, so I safeworded and we talked about it, and then the next time when he asked me to do it, I was able to trust that, even though it still scared me, he would be there for me and that if it did get to be too much, he'd stop if I safeworded again. My using my safeword made us even closer."

Derek thought that made sense, though he didn't think he would have understood it before. "It deepened the trust between you."

"It did. That doesn't mean that a relationship where the safeword is never used isn't just as trusting and meaningful. It just means that using your safeword isn't a bad thing."

"That's good to know. When I first read about it and Luke explained it more to me, I thought it would be a bad thing to make you safeword, but it's not, is it? It's just a thing that means I trust you."

"You're a fast learner. It's like you were meant to be a Dom all along."

Derek thought Sawyer was pretty happy about that.

"Like it was waiting for you to come along to wake it up." He couldn't imagine being a Dom for anybody else. "So what other stuff are you into? What about whips and chains and stuff—those are the things most people think of when you say BDSM, I think."

"Well, I've never really been into pain for pain's sake. If you want to try it out, though, I'm not going to say no. Doms and subs are partners. It shouldn't be all one-sided."

Derek took a deep breath as relief flooded through him. "I'm not sure I could deliberately hurt you," he admitted.

"Well then, as I'm not a pain slut, that works out just fine. I'm a size queen and into ass play. Which I may have already mentioned…."

Derek laughed. Sawyer knew damn well he'd mentioned it. Hell, they'd played from that for days over their long weekend. He decided to play along. "I'll have to keep that in mind."

Sawyer pounced, arms wrapping around his neck as Sawyer kissed him. He kissed Sawyer right back, pleased at the outcome of their discussion. He was so glad he'd asked, because it had been weighing on his mind since Luke had brought it up.

"Is it weird?" he asked. "Being the one with the experience and sort of having to teach me how to be a Dom?"

"We all have to start from somewhere, Derek. I love that you're working so hard to learn how to be the perfect Dom for me. And as long as I know it's what you want too, I have no problem guiding you through it. In fact, I think it's a wonderful way for us to learn each other."

"I want it." Derek didn't want Sawyer to have any doubts about that. "I love being your Dom." He wouldn't do it for anyone else, but it felt right and good with Sawyer.

"I think that's wonderful for both of us."

"It is." Derek couldn't agree more.

"Master…?" Sawyer looked up into his eyes again.

"What is it?"

"My ass has been empty since you took the plug out Monday morning, and I'm still sensitive enough that everything I touch makes me need. Please help me."

"Did any of the plugs we ordered Friday afternoon come in?"

Sawyer moaned loudly and nodded. "I took them out of their packages and washed them. They've been taunting me since they came yesterday."

Derek's cock, already half-hard from his lapful of Sawyer, went fully hard in a matter of seconds. He groaned as it pushed against the zipper of his jeans. He shouldn't have gone commando. Of course he wasn't complaining that much about the slight bite from the metal.

"I want you to suck me off first. Then you can bring me the one that you want most to try, and I'll put it in before we eat."

Sawyer wriggled on his lap. "Thank you, Master."

Then Sawyer slid to the floor between Derek's legs. He spread himself as wide as he could in the easy chair and curled his fingers at his sides. Sawyer licked his own lips as he popped the top button and began carefully working down the zipper. As soon as it was free, Derek's cock popped out of the jeans, actually hitting Sawyer's cheek. Moaning, Sawyer turned his head, taking Derek's cock right in.

The tight suction felt amazing. There was no teasing, no drawing it out—Sawyer sucked and bobbed his head, tongue lashing at Derek's prick, playing with the slit every time only the tip of his cock remained between Sawyer's lips. It seemed Sawyer was eager to get him off so they could move on to the plug portion of the evening. Considering it had been three days and Derek knew how much Sawyer craved being filled, he couldn't blame Sawyer for trying to make it quick.

It wasn't like he was getting shorted. The full-on, make-you-come blow job felt incredible. Derek finally grabbed hold of Sawyer's head, holding on as Sawyer made his balls hug his body, the ache in them delicious. He made himself keep his eyes open so he could watch Sawyer's head bob over his cock, the look of pleasure on Sawyer's face making Derek enjoy it all the more. Sawyer might like ass play the best, but he obviously loved sucking too.

The treat of teeth as Sawyer pulled up had Derek gasping, and he came, his balls pumping his spunk into Sawyer's mouth. He shuddered as Sawyer continued to pull at his cock, sending delightful aftershocks through him. Then Sawyer carefully cleaned him, taking his time to make sure Derek had the full experience. Such a giving, sweet man.

Derek finally ran his hand through Sawyer's hair, pushing it off his face. "God, you're good at that. Thank you."

Sawyer licked an errant drop of come from the corner of his lips. "My pleasure."

"No, I'm pretty sure it was more my pleasure." Derek laughed. It felt so good, being with Sawyer. "It's your turn—go get one of the plugs." He was curious which one Sawyer was going to pick—which one most intrigued his experienced lover.

"Yes, Sir. I've opened the drawer to look at one of them quite a few times." Sawyer stood and went toward the bedroom. Derek watched, memorizing how Sawyer walked because he knew it would look different once Sawyer had the plug in.

Sawyer came back a moment later with the tub of lube and one of the dildos. His cock was hard, a dark red, and even from across the room, Derek could see that Sawyer was leaking, his excitement was so high. He turned his attention from Sawyer's cock to the one Sawyer was carrying. For this plug was cock-shaped. More or less.

It was long and thick, with several twists in it, and the end tapered to a rounded point, the bottom of the top two inches flat and covered in ridges. The inch and a half or so before the base of the thing was covered all around in suction cups. It was so pretty and so interesting, and Derek had to admit, he'd been worried it would be too much but had put it in the cart and bought it anyway.

"This is the one you want to use first?" He had to admit to being excited about that.

"Uh-huh. It was intriguing enough in the pictures, but for real?" Sawyer moaned, his fingers moving over the massive thing. "I love all the different textures and can't wait to feel them inside me." Sawyer offered it to him.

Derek took the plug and slid his fingers over it, feeling the ridges at the top, exploring the twists, and testing the suction cups at the bottom. They actually worked as suction cups—how was that going to feel on the inside of Sawyer's ass? He could see that Sawyer was excited to find out.

He ran the ridges at the tip up and down along Sawyer's cock, and several new drops of clear liquid came out of the slit, drooling down the sides. Then Derek pressed the suction cups against Sawyer's balls and slowly pulled the plug away from them. The suction cups stuck, tugging on Sawyer's ball sac, pulling it away from his body for a moment. Sawyer shuddered and moaned as they suddenly let go.

"Oh God. Master. Please."

"Time to insert this bad boy."

"Yes, please, Master."

He took the lube from Sawyer. "Over my knees."

Sawyer didn't need to be asked twice, moving quickly to drape himself over Derek's lap. Derek helped to make sure Sawyer's cock was between his legs.

Sawyer's hands wrapped around his calf. "I'm going to come like this, Master."

He thought about that for a moment, rubbing at Sawyer's ass. "You're allowed to come while we do this. But after that you won't be able to come until after we've eaten and probably played some more."

"Yes, Master. Thank you, Master."

He grabbed the lube and got his fingers slick. Then he rubbed them against Sawyer's sweet hole. It tried to grab at them, to pull them in, but Derek wasn't ready for that yet. He was doing this his way. Which is what Sawyer wanted anyway, he knew that. Even if his pet did have a greedy ass. Pet. He did like how that sounded. It emphasized the "mine" part of how he felt about Sawyer.

"Be patient, pet. I'll give you what you need."

Sawyer moaned and shivered. "Please, Master. Thank you."

Derek grabbed a bunch more lube on the tip of his fingers and used two to push the gel into Sawyer's hole. It needed to be very wet and slippery for this big plug to go in. Sawyer's hands tightened on his calf, and a low, steady moan sounded. He loved that he was drawing those wanton noises out of Sawyer. Clearly, he was doing something right.

Putting yet more lube on his fingers, he pushed the gel and his fingers in this time, going in as deep as he could. He loved how hot and tight Sawyer was around him, and how silky smooth those inner walls were. It was like being invited into a magical place. He made himself go slowly, made himself take his time. He knew it would be better if he let the anticipation build, if Sawyer was already wild and needing before he used the plug at all. With that in mind, he fingerfucked Sawyer slowly, scissoring his fingers apart and twisting them together as he pushed in and out. When he found Sawyer's gland, he touched it a few times, the poor little button of pleasure still fairly sensitive after the milking. Sawyer jerked and moaned, dancing on his fingers like a puppet.

Finally, he felt that Sawyer was open enough and sensitive enough to appreciate the silicone plug with all its different textures.

He pulled his fingers out and teased the tip of the plug in. The point was barely as thick as his little finger, but it grew bigger quickly, more than three fingers wide by the time the second inch was through. He pulled it out and fed it in again, repeating the motions so that Sawyer got the full benefit of all the little ridges the head boasted.

Sawyer was soon moving with him, rocking on his legs as one moan after another poured out of him. Sawyer's cock was leaking, wetting Derek's thighs with slow, consistent drops. Derek pushed the plug in farther, knowing the ridges would be as wonderful deeper in as they had been just inside Sawyer's opening. Sawyer's moans continued as Derek fed the plug into him. He kept going until he got to the end with its suction cups.

Moving wildly, Sawyer rocked between his legs and pushed back for more of the plug, soft panting and wailing words begging for more coming constantly.

"You're amazing," he told Sawyer as he put pressure on the base of the plug and watched Sawyer take those last couple of inches in by himself.

"For you, Master." Sawyer moaned and bucked, the plug sinking in all the way.

Derek grabbed the base and tugged, pulling the plug out until only the first couple of inches remained inside Sawyer. Then he began the slow job of sending the plug deep once again. And again, Sawyer helped, bucking and writhing.

This time, Derek gave it a minute and then began to twist the plug, the suction cups tugging on Sawyer's skin before suddenly letting go and attaching to a new patch of skin. Sawyer cried out and increased his rocking, fucking Derek's legs hard and fast. He came with a cry with the plug buried deep inside, spunk splashing over Derek's legs, the scent rising on the air, making him harder than ever too.

Sawyer rested his head against Derek's thigh, hands clinging to Derek's calf as he panted. "Oh God. That was… is…. God."

Derek beamed, so pleased he'd taken the chance to include this plug among their purchases. "I'm glad it was good because you won't be able to come again until later. Much later." He twisted the plug, knowing the ridges and suction cups had to be leaving incredible sensations inside of Sawyer.

Sawyer keened for him, head coming up and the panting increased. "That's so good. I've never felt anything like it."

"Cool." He kept playing with the plug, thrusting with it, twisting it, mixing it all up so the sensations kept changing.

"No, hot," Sawyer managed to say around renewed panting.

Derek laughed softly, tickled by the reply and so happy with what they were doing and the way it got to Sawyer.

Finally, his stomach got through to his brain, and he had to stop because he was hungry and the place smelled like an amazing restaurant. He seated the plug and patted Sawyer's ass, pleased with how wide a surface the base of the plug was. He was going to enjoy watching Sawyer squirming on those hard kitchen chairs. No sitting in his lap to feed each other this evening. At least not until dessert.

He bent and placed a kiss on each asscheek, then tapped the base of the plug, watching as a shudder moved through Sawyer.

"Time for supper. I'm sure you're as hungry as I am."

"I am hungry, Master. Though more for things other than food," Sawyer added in a mutter.

"For those things you'll have to wait." Derek helped Sawyer up.

"Yes, Master, I serve at your pleasure."

Derek got up and followed Sawyer to the kitchen, moaning at the way Sawyer moved with that plug up his ass. Damn. It seemed no matter what Sawyer did—it was all Derek's pleasure.

CHAPTER FIFTEEN

SAWYER LAY in bed, listening to the breathing of the three men he shared it with. He should get up and get breakfast going, but he wanted to take a few moments to revel in the fact that he had this. A new master. Another master and sub to play with, to make things even better, deeper. Someone out there was looking out for him, making sure he connected with the people he needed.

Derek grumbled softly and pulled him closer, still mostly asleep, though Sawyer now recognized the move as Derek slowly waking up. How much did he love the fact that Derek's first instinct on becoming conscious was to hold Sawyer closer? He touched Derek's cheek, fingers lingering. Such a wonderful man. Who cared for him so well.

It was true that he'd worried Derek was only taking on the Dominant role because that's what he thought Sawyer needed, but over the last weeks, Derek had demonstrated a knack for it—and more, a joy in it that Sawyer couldn't deny. Luke still occasionally lent a guiding hand, but Derek read and researched and wasn't afraid to ask Sawyer what he liked, what he wanted. A Dom who knew he didn't know everything and who expected to work *with* his sub was a wonderful treasure.

Derek nuzzled his cheek and pooched his lips for a kiss. Chuckling, Sawyer pressed their lips together. One kiss turned into another, and they shared air, shared their feelings through the soft glide of their lips. When they finally parted, Derek opened his eyes and smiled down at Sawyer.

"God, I love you."

Sawyer felt warmth rush through him at the words. He felt even more warmth when Derek didn't try to take it back or bluster his way through having not meant to say it.

"I'm falling for you too," he told Derek. It was true. He knew what love felt like. It colored everything.

"You don't have to say it back."

"But I want to." Love made everything better.

"You guys move fast," murmured Benny.

Sawyer shook his head. Compared to him and James, this had been slow. Derek had to do the work of cracking through Sawyer's armor, built up in the wake of James's death. "We've moved at just the right speed."

"Good answer," noted Luke. "And congratulations, you two. That's a damn good place to be—in love."

Derek chuckled and rubbed their noses together. "I love you," he said again, whispering it this time.

"I love you," Sawyer answered. A blanket of comfort and happiness settled around him. This was right. Derek and he were right.

"We should mark the occasion," Luke suggested, giving his and Derek's shoulders a pat. "Any ideas, Derek?"

"Uh, well, I sort of do have an idea." Derek looked into his eyes. "I was thinking it's the kind of thing you mark with a ring. But it's not like we've gotten engaged or are getting married. Not that we aren't doing either of those, just not right now."

Sawyer waited patiently while Derek babbled, knowing he'd get to the crux of what he wanted to say soon enough.

"I would like to give you a ring, but not one for your hand."

Oh. Sawyer's breath caught in his throat, his heart beginning to beat faster.

"I'd like to give you one here." Derek grabbed his cock and squeezed the tip.

Fuck yes. Sawyer moaned, his ass squeezing hard around the plug he wore. "Please. Please, Master, I would love that."

"Where's he getting a ring?" Benny demanded.

"I can guess," murmured Luke. "And I think it's a great idea. I know the right guy to do it too. Will you let us come and watch?"

Derek checked in with him with another gaze into his eyes, then smiled and nodded. "Yeah, we could all go. You guys would be like our best men in kinkitude."

Benny cackled, and Derek gave him a sheepish grin, the expression turning tickled as Sawyer began laughing too.

"Will there be a ceremony?" Sawyer asked. "Because I'll totally vow to take you as mine in kinkitude for as long as we both shall live."

"Shouldn't it be for as long as you can both still get it up?" Benny asked.

Derek didn't miss a beat before answering, "Nope. That's what plugs are for."

Sawyer kissed him, their laughter shared between them. This was something special he shared with Derek, the joy in just being together— it was always right there near the surface with this sweet man.

"I should get breakfast going." He had three hungry men to feed, four if he counted himself.

"It can wait." Derek kissed him, making it clear what the breakfast would be waiting for.

Sawyer could live with that.

CHAPTER SIXTEEN

DEREK COULDN'T quite believe they were doing this. Okay, he was here, in the piercer's back room with Sawyer and Luke and Benny, and Sawyer's dick was out, already half-hard as they waited, so clearly they were going to do it. They were going to pierce Sawyer's cock. Well, the piercer was. He and the guys were going to watch.

They were doing it because of him, though. Because he'd wanted to do something to mark them coming together and saying I love you for the first time. That was big. And a ring in Sawyer's cock was pretty damn big too. The physical equivalent of saying I love you. Derek had even picked out the ring he wanted. The thickness of the rose gold mitigated the possible girlieness of the color—though only Benny had called it girlie. Sawyer had just looked at him with adoration in his eyes. Sawyer always made him feel like the King of the World.

He squeezed Sawyer's hand as the piercer—Origami was the guy's name, and Derek was pretty sure it was not the name he'd been born with—came in and closed the door behind him. Sawyer squeezed back and gave him an excited grin.

Derek looked over at Benny, who was in Luke's lap. "I gotta admit, I'm not sure I could do that."

"It's not a contest," Luke pointed out.

"No, it's not." Sawyer reached out with his free hand, and Benny took it. "We need different things, and there's nothing wrong with that. In fact, it makes it better, doesn't it? That we're not all the same."

Grinning, Benny squeezed Sawyer's hand. "Yeah, yeah. You're just so *nice*."

"I'm not sure if that was a compliment or an insult," Sawyer noted, though he didn't seem the least bit upset.

"That's the joy of Benny." Luke laughed and gave Sawyer's hand a pat. "Thank you for including us in this. Both of you."

"You're a part of us." Derek knew Sawyer felt the same way. They'd talked about it one night, about how they were definitely a couple, but that Luke and Benny were an important part of their life together.

Benny beamed, but Luke gave them a serious look. "We're very lucky that we have friends who are lovers too and who understand how we can all fit together, be better because of each other. Four people means more love to share, not less to go around."

"Amen," said Origami, rolling the tray he'd been stocking next to Sawyer. "Are you ready for this?"

Sawyer nodded without hesitation. "I am."

"Me too." Derek gave Sawyer a quick kiss, then leaned his head on the chair, looking down at Sawyer's cock, which was now completely hard.

"I might come," Sawyer whispered.

"You're allowed," he whispered back. Sawyer squeezed his hand again.

Origami grabbed a felt pen and made a mark on Sawyer's penis. "I'm going to do it here. Are you happy with the placement?"

All four of them leaned in and looked, but it was Derek who said yes. Sawyer only nodded after he'd given his approval.

"All right, then. Did you want me to use the numbing cream?"

"Oh no." Sawyer shook his head. "I want to be able to feel."

"It's not permanent. It should wear off in about an hour." Origami waved the tube around, but Sawyer shook his head. Again.

"I'm good. Just do it."

"You got it." Origami worked quickly, gloved hand holding Sawyer's cock steady as he pushed the needle through Sawyer's skin, the ring attached following it right through.

Benny squeaked, and Derek's stomach leaped into his throat for a moment, but then it was done, and Sawyer cried out, his hips bucking as come poured out of his slit. Sawyer relaxed back in his seat with a moan.

"Nice one," murmured Origami. "I'll give you guys some privacy—my next appointment isn't for forty-five minutes." Then he slipped from the room, leaving the four of them alone.

Derek took a look, admiring the soft gold as it glinted in Sawyer's skin, the scent of Sawyer's come strong on the air.

"Oh my God. That is incredible. It's beautiful too." And Derek was more in love than ever.

Sawyer reached up and cupped his cheek, and he brought their mouths together, putting all the things he was feeling into the kiss. Then they rested their foreheads together, breathing in the same air.

It was Luke who grabbed a wet wipe from Origami's tray and cleaned Sawyer up.

"Thanks, dude." Derek was too busy eye-fucking Sawyer right now.

"Anytime."

"So when do we get to play with it?" Benny wanted to know.

"Not for a while." Derek wasn't too busy to look again at the pamphlet for aftercare they'd been given. "And we'll need to keep it clean whenever liquid comes out of it." He gave Sawyer a grin. "I'll have to milk you on a regular basis so that there's a onetime cleanup every few days."

Sawyer's eyes went wide; then he moaned and pushed against Derek's chest.

"Maybe we can watch the next time you do that. Then the time after, I can do Benny at the same time."

"I don't know about that," murmured Benny. "Sawyer was seriously losing it when you did that to him."

"Only in the best way." Sawyer sighed. "Can we go home? I'm going to need a couple Advil soon, and I'd rather be done traveling before the adrenaline wears off completely."

"Of course!" Derek carefully tucked Sawyer back into his underwear, then pulled his sweats up. God, he loved this man. He looked into Sawyer's eyes. They still pulled him in, but the sadness that had been there when they first met was gone now, and he could see his own happiness reflected back at him.

He helped Sawyer to stand, and Luke and Benny went out ahead of them like a pair of bodyguards. Derek held Sawyer's hand as they walked to the car. This was better than ice cream. Even pecan caramel brittle.

Often referred to as "Space Cowboy" and "Gangsta of Love" while still striving for the moniker of "Maurice," SEAN MICHAEL spends his days surfing, smutting, organizing his immense gourd collection and fantasizing about one day retiring on a small secluded island peopled entirely by horseshoe crabs. While collecting vast amounts of vintage gay pulp novels and mood rings, Sean whiles away the hours between dropping the f-bomb and pursuing the *Kama Sutra* by channeling the long-lost spirit of John Wayne and singing along with the soundtrack to *Chicago*.

A longtime writer of complicated haiku, currently Sean is attempting to learn the advanced arts of plate spinning and soap carving sex toys.

Barring any of that? He'll stick with writing his stories, thanks, and rubbing pretty bodies together to see if they spark.

Website: www.seanmichaelwrites.com
Blog: seanmichaelwrites.blogspot.ca
Facebook: www.facebook.com/SeanMichaelWrites
Twitter: @seanmichael09
Instagram: www.instagram.com/seanmichaelpics

BASES
LOADED

SEAN MICHAEL

Can they survive the off-season and keep from striking out?

Baseball player Brett must get rehabilitation for his shoulder if he wants another season in the Major Leagues. He and his partner, Benj, take off to the boonies to stay with physical therapist Ralph, a tough-talking, routine-setting guy, and Jean, Ralph's Cajun lover, who cooks as well as he loves.

Brett and Ralph butt heads from the beginning. Ralph wants Brett to be more in touch with his feelings; Brett wants Ralph to give him his therapy and leave him alone. Benj and Jean get along far better, with Jean showing Benj around the kitchen and reassuring him when things with Brett get strained.

Before Ralph can even begin to work on Brett's shoulder, though, Brett faces an even more difficult physical challenge, one that does more than threaten his career. He and Benj have to work through some tough issues, making decisions that will affect the rest of their lives together. Their gradual friendship with Ralph and Jean helps them through the bad times, but even that might not be enough to pull them through

www.dreamspinnerpress.com

SEAN MICHAEL

DADDY,
DADDY,
AND ME

When Jeff agreed to be the sperm donor to his best friend Beth, he never expected a tragedy to leave his newborn and three-year-old motherless. Beth's loss has totally thrown his life into chaos: his lover has left him, his house isn't anywhere near childproof, and his boss feels the restaurant has been patient enough with Jeff's time off.

Donny has always known he wanted to work with kids, and he just finished his degree in early childhood education. He didn't count on the prejudice he'd face as not only a male nanny, but a gay one at that. Job-hunting has been frustrating to say the least, so when he knocks on Jeff's door and is greeted by the sounds of things breaking and a pair of screaming children, he thinks maybe he can begin this particular interview with a trial by fire.

Becoming the nanny to Jeff's children might be a dream come true for Danny and exactly what Jeff needs, but are either of them ready to really be a family?

www.dreamspinnerpress.com

Daddy
Needs a Date

SEAN MICHAEL

With four girls, single dad Ryan Withers has his hands too full to look for romance. He's not complaining—he loves his daughter and the three nieces he adopted when their parents died, and he would do anything for them. He's caught off guard when his mother and daughter decide to play matchmaker.

Alex Bernot works in disaster relief, his job taking him all over the world, helping others, for extended periods of time. He's staying with his aunt while he's home, and she sets him up on a blind date. Finding a special someone isn't really on his mind, but he goes to make his aunt happy.

Ryan and Alex enjoy each other's company more than either of them expected, and they soon make a second date. Their lives are complicated, though, in very different ways, and soon family needs and their jobs conspire to pull them apart. They'll need to figure out how to work through the things keeping them apart, but first they'll have to decide if they even want to....

www.dreamspinnerpress.com

DREAMSPUN
BEYOND

THE SUPERS

Sean Michael

The Supers

Hunting ghosts and finding
more than they bargained for.

The Supers

Hunting ghosts and finding more than they bargained for.

Blaine Franks is a member of the paranormal research group the Supernatural Explorers. When the group loses their techie to a cross-country move, newly graduated Flynn Huntington gets the job. Flynn fits in with the guys right off the bat, but when it comes to him and Blaine, it's more than just getting along.

Things heat up between Blaine and Flynn as they explore their first haunted building, an abandoned hospital, together. Their relationship isn't all that progresses, though, and soon it seems that an odd bite on Blaine's neck has become much more.

Hitchhiking ghosts, a tragic love story forgotten by time, and the mystery of room 204 round out a romance where the things that go bump in the night are real.

www.dreamspinnerpress.com

UNLIKELY
HERO

Sean Michael

When his three-year-old daughter is kidnapped, Eric Wilson doesn't have many options, and time is running out. With nowhere else to turn, he reaches out to his ex, influential businessman Brock Vencenza, whose money and contacts might be able to save Josie.

Brock never got over Eric's loss, and he's more than willing to help when Eric needs him most. Together with law enforcement and private security, they embark on a twisting investigation to find the little girl—and who wants to hurt her and destroy both men in the process. Under the circumstances, confessing he still has feelings for Eric would be inappropriate, but Brock can't deny what's in his heart. He doesn't know if their love can be rekindled or if he can even protect Eric and Josie. But one thing is certain: Brock's determined to be the hero in reality that he is in Eric's eyes.

www.dreamspinnerpress.com